DENNIS

in  STAR PAWS

THE RISE OF MINNIE

D0680041

A STUDIO PRESS BOOK

First published in the UK in 2020 by Studio Press,
an imprint of Bonnier Books UK,
The Plaza, 535 King's Road, London SW10 0SZ

www.studiopressbooks.co.uk
www.beano.com

A Beano Studios Product © D.C. Thomson Ltd 2020

Written and illustrated by Nigel Auchterlounie

All rights reserved. No part of this publication may be
reproduced or transmitted in any form or by any means,
electronic or mechanical, including photocopy, recording,
or any information storage and retrieval system,
without prior permission in writing from the publisher.

2 4 6 8 10 9 7 5 3 1

All rights reserved
Paperback: 978-1-78741-551-5

A CIP catalogue record for this book
is available from the British Library.
Printed and bound by Clays Ltd, Elcograf S.p.A.

AN EPIC BEANO® ADVENTURE
DENNIS
in STAR PAWS
THE RISE OF MINNIE

STUDIO PRESS

PREVIOUSLY IN BEANOTOWN – A SHORT HISTORY LESSON

I know what you're thinking (if you're anything like Dennis). **Urrrrgh! History?!** It's bad enough that I'm being made to read a book, but this book's got history in it!

Well, I'm sorry about that.

But don't worry, I'm not going to go through everything that's ever happened in Beanotown.

I'll not talk about the asteroid that killed the dinosaurs landing there. Or mention that there are still some dinosaurs living on the island in the middle of the duck pond.

I'll also not mention the Vikings who first visited Beanotown before there was a town there at all, and how they found a crystal skull that gave them headaches and strange ideas when they looked at it (though that does crop up later).

I'll not go into any detail about the clock on

top of the town hall that is actually a time machine. (That **doesn't** crop up later.)

Instead, we'll fast forward to Victorian times – 1851, to be exact. When Beanotown really became Beanotown...

The Beano brothers, Barry and Brian, moved their toy and pranks factory there from London, and built most of what's known today as "the old town" to house the factory workers. Brian Beano was the sensible brother, and he concerned himself with the day-to-day business of running a factory. **Boring!** Who wants to know about sensible people?

His brother Barry, however, was quite the opposite... As he was extremely rich, we'll call him "eccentric" instead of weird.

Barry Beano was obsessed with games and puzzles. He even built the town and its streets as one giant puzzle. Today, people who've lived there all their lives still get lost in the old town from time to time. And if you attempt to drive through the area, it won't be long before your satnav starts saying things like, "Er, hold on, I could have sworn it was this way!"

You see, Barry's hero was Daedalus. In Greek mythology, Daedalus built the Labyrinth to hold the terrible half-man, half-bull creature known as the Minotaur. It's thought that the roads of Beanotown are based on a plan of the Labyrinth, though Barry didn't do this to keep a terrible monster from

6

escaping – he did it for a laugh.

Barry was a builder and an inventor. One time he nearly succeeded in building a dinosaur park on Duck Island. It's possible you may have heard about that. He also created the time machine on top of the town hall – but as I say, that's not a part of this story. But perhaps his most ambitious, outlandish invention lay undiscovered beneath Beanotown...

A THIRD BOOK?
WHEN WILL THEY LEARN?

There are some good things about being an author: swanning around coffee shops, lying on the couch, "thinking", telling people you're an author, and that one of your books was a bestseller for more than twenty minutes. Stuff like that.

The bad thing about being an author, though, is that publishers do keep insisting that you write books!

And writing wordy book goodly is hard.

Not long ago, I awoke with a start in the dead of night. There was a terrible storm outside. I looked at the clock by my bed. It was three o'clock in the morning. Lightning struck, and I saw the familiar figure of my publisher sitting on an unfamiliar armchair at the end of my bed.

Turning on my bedside lamp, I rubbed my eyes.

"It's that time again, my dear boy," she said coldly, brushing an imaginary crumb from her knee. She wanted another book.

"Are we absolutely sure I'm the best person to do this?" I asked.

"Of course you're not!" my publisher readily agreed. "But we need another book. One featuring that Dennis boy and his dog," she continued. "Oh and put that girl in it too. She tests well in our focus groups. They like her attitude."

She fixed me with one of her icy stares.

"Okay?"

None of this was okay, not at all. But what could I do? I nodded.

"Excellent," she replied with a curt smile. "Keep the chair. So long!"

Then the light went out, and the room was plunged into darkness once more. I got up to switch the main light on, turned, and saw that she had gone, leaving the empty armchair behind.

(The encounter was deeply disturbing, but the chair's lovely.)

SANTA?! IN SUMMER?

I woke early the next morning, from a fitful sleep.

I'm no good at coming up with story ideas myself. The other two books were based on tales told to me by Dennis Menace (his surname is **Menace**). So I'd come to rely on him – and if you've ever met Dennis, you'll know how unreliable he is.

I thought for a moment... I would have to—

But at that moment, my house was shaken by an almighty thud and the sound of breaking glass. It felt like something very big had crashed into the front of my house. By the sounds of it, the living-room window had not survived.

I threw on my dressing gown and ran downstairs. Before I got to the bottom step, a deer of some sort staggered out of the living room in a cloud of dust. It shook its head and squinted at me, looking dazed and confused, before staggering into the kitchen.

"That was your fault!" came a familiar voice from the living room.

Dennis! I thought, and hurried in.

"My fault?!" bellowed a rather large, bearded man in a red velvet suit. He was standing in the wreckage that had once been my living room. "You were driving!" he finished.

"Santa?" I asked, not quite believing what I was seeing.

Santa looked at me furiously.

I took a step back. I knew he wasn't angry with me, but I thought it would still be a good idea to keep my distance. Santa is a magical being, after all – what if he had laser beam eyes or something?

Dennis saw me and rolled *his* eyes. "What do you want?"

"What do you mean, what do I want?" I blurted. "You've crashed Santa's sleigh into my living room!"

"Chill. Santa's elves will fix all this in minutes," Dennis assured me.

"But how did it happen?" I asked.

"How did what happen?" asked Santa.

"Well... you crashing into my house, in the middle of summer!" I replied. There's probably a story there, I was thinking. Maybe I can use that for my new book.

Santa clenched his fists, gritted his teeth, and fixed me with his most threatening look. "This never happened."

He always seems so friendly in the shopping centre.

I looked around at my devastated living room, complete with a sleigh sticking out through the window. "It sort of does look like it happened," I pointed out.

Dennis stepped forwards. "This is one of those secret deals. The story of how this happened," he said, waving his hands around at the destruction, "and what me and Sants have to do next can never be told. Top secret government stuff, you understand?" He tapped the side of his nose and winked at me.

It was then I saw my chance. "In that case, I do need a favour. I need another story. Immediately!"

"Deal. What about the time I went to space, and had a space battle and everything? Do you want to hear about that?"

I did, but remembering what my publisher had said, I asked, "Are Gnasher and Minnie in it too?"

"Of course Gnasher's in it!" Dennis assured me. "And Minnie did some stuff too."

"Good," I answered, pulling my lucky notepad from my dressing-gown pocket, brushing the broken glass and rubble off the sofa, and making myself comfortable between Dennis and Santa. "Tell me all about it."

A MASSIVE BLOCK OF PASTA

It was a day like any other day in Beanotown. The sun was shining a little more than is usual, as it normally does there. The birds were cheeping in their nests, a little more than in the average town. And the butcher's van left the road and floated up to the huge electromagnet hanging over the bridge, like it doesn't do anywhere else.

Walter laughed his most evil laugh.

He'd been busy. He'd borrowed a magnet crane from the local scrapyard and had turned the bridge on Main Street into a toll road.

The idea was simple: pay five pounds to cross the bridge (under the magnet) or else.

The butcher wasn't keen on paying the new toll, so Walter had gleefully turned the magnet on.

He lifted the van up high, the winch – the part of the crane that wound the cable – clicking and clanking loudly under the strain. Walter then swung the van off the bridge, over the river, and laughed some more.

"Ready to pay?" he asked again, dangling the meat-filled van over the edge.

"Not so fast!" said Dennis.

Unbelievably, Walter hadn't noticed Dennis approach. He was in a very similar machine, only this one had a wrecking ball dangling from the end of its crane instead of a giant magnet. The wrecking ball had a picture of Dennis's face scrawled on it.

There was supposed to be some more hero-villain chat. That's how Dennis had thought it would play out, at least, but without hesitation Walter turned off the magnet, dropping the van into the river, and swung the huge magnet around to clash into Dennis's wrecking ball.

Splash! went the van...

Well, the front two wheels went splash. The back wheels went splotch as they landed in the mud. Beanotown "River" is pretty much a stream. The water only came halfway up the front wheels.

CLANG! The magnet and the wrecking ball clashed together.

Nearby, Minnie was watching, licking a blue

lolly. She turned to the woman standing next to her. "It's a bit like giant conkers, isn't it?" she said. "Only, one of the conkers is a big magnet. So not really."

Walter swung the magnet over the nearest car, turned the magnet on, picked the car up and swung it at Dennis.

Crash! The car smashed into the wrecking ball, and the wrecking ball... wrecked it.

With Gnasher sitting next to him in the cabin, Dennis crunched the gears on the wrecking ball, swung it back... and his mum banged on the window and called him in for tea.

"I'm kind of in the middle of something here!" he protested to his mother, who'd come out to find him. She was stood on the caterpillar tracks of the crane and had a smudge of dirt on her cheek.

"It'll not keep," his mum shouted through the glass. "It's pasta. Pasta sticks together if you leave it. It never reheats right."

Gnasher rolled his eyes. To his mind, pasta wasn't right even before you reheat it, because pasta's not sausages.

"It'll be fine!" Dennis said. "I don't mind if it's a massive solid block of pasta!"

Walter started laughing. "Run along home to Mother!" he sneered.

"Walter, your dinner's ready!" Walter's mum shouted from the other side of the road.

Walter rolled his eyes. "But—" Walter started, knowing he wasn't going to win, but feeling like he at least had to try.

"But nothing!" his mum said, in her "Don't mess" tone. "You can play conkers with your friend after. He's got to go in too."

"He's not my friend!" Dennis and Walter both protested.

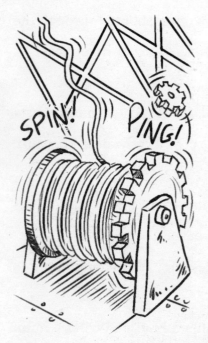

SPIN!

PING!

Minnie laughed.

From behind her, her mother said, "Have you been spoiling your appetite with those blue lollies again?"

Dennis took advantage of this distraction. He swung the wrecking ball. Before Walter could do anything about it – **CLANG!** – the wrecking ball hit the magnet so hard the cable winch holding it up snapped with a **PING!**

The cable winch is the bit that winds the cable up and down – so when it broke the cable quickly unravelled and the magnet dropped noisily to the pavement.

Walter wrestled with the controls and scowled. He couldn't lift it again, but he did manage to turn it back on.

The magnet scraped along the flagstones and attached itself – with a **KUNG!** – to one of those green metal cupboards you often see on the street. Sparks flew from the magnet, and the electrical box made a **ZOOP!** sound.

"Okay, this is **OVER!"** Dennis's mum announced.

And so it was. Which is quite an unsatisfactory way for a Dennis-Walter battle to end.

Everything went back to normal – well, as normal as you get for Beanotown – and Dennis and Gnasher went home for tea. (You'll be glad to know that there was a sausage for Gnasher.)

TURN IT OFF AND ON AGAIN

Something was wrong. Deeply and profoundly wrong.

Extremely and exceedingly and greatly and immensely and enormously and terribly and tremendously and awfully and intensely and thoroughly wrong.

The Wi-Fi wasn't working.

Dennis shook his tablet vigorously.

25

"IT'S LIKE LIVING IN ROMAN TIMES!" Dennis shouted at his bedroom ceiling.

Gnasher, lying at the foot of his bed, lifted an ear but didn't open his eyes. This didn't seem to be anything sausage-related, so it didn't concern him.

"DAAAAAAAAAAD! The Wi-Fi's not

working," Dennis yelled at the top of his voice.

"TURN IT OFF AND ON AGAIN, THEN!" Dad yelled from some other part of the house. But the router thing wasn't in Dennis's bedroom.

"YOU'RE NEARER!" Dennis shouted back, not knowing if it was true or not.

"I DON'T NEED THE WI-FI RESET!"

Dad shouted in reply, from wherever he was.

"WHY CAN'T ANYONE HAVE A NORMAL CONVERSATION IN THIS HOUSE, WITHOUT SHOUTING?!" Mum shout-asked from a third, unknown location.

Dennis got up and angrily stormed downstairs.

The router was in the living room. On the way, Dennis found Mum in the hall, under a sea of shoes and boots.

"I want noise-cancelling headphones for my birthday," Mum said randomly.

"Noise-cancelling?" Dennis asked.

"Fancy headphones that cancel out noises," Mum told him.

"Okay... What are you doing, Mum?" Dennis asked.

"Isn't it obvious?!" she said. **"I'm trying to tidy this mess!"**

Upstairs, Gnasher frowned at all of this. He was trying to sleep – to access, hopefully, some sort of sausage-related dream. (You don't need Wi-Fi for dreams.) But his hearing was ten times better than human hearing, and all the shouting was making it impossible.

A NOISE I DON'T KNOW HOW TO SPELL

A similar scene was being played out at Minnie's house. Minnie was a bit less glued to screens than Dennis, but the moment she found out the Wi-Fi wasn't working, being on it was all she could think about.

She sat on the sofa and made a series of bored noises.

URRRGH! was the first noise. **HUMF!** was another. Minnie even made a noise by sighing loudly out of her nose (which I don't know how to spell.)

I really need some noise-cancelling headphones, Minnie's dad thought.

He saw that Minnie was bored, and usually when Minnie was bored something in the house would get broken. It was always an accident, but still... So he shooed her out of the house.

Let something I don't own get broken for once, he thought.

Minnie wandered aimlessly for a while, and she found herself on the golf course. She was stood on one of the really nicely mowed bits that have the hole you're meant to get the ball into.

The hole, Minnie saw, had a flag in it. And flags really want you to pick them up and twizz them around. I mean, they're flags! So moments after spotting it, Minnie was twizzing it around. At first she tried a flag-waving style, which quickly turned into fighting imaginary aliens.

"Take that!" Minnie shouted at one imaginary foe. "You can get lost an' all!" she warned another non-existent alien baddie, as she swished at them with the golf flag.

It took quite a bit of effort to vanquish all the imaginary baddies, but Minnie managed it.

She stood tall on the pile of imaginary alien bad guys and held the flag high above her head in victory.

"Hey!" shouted one of the aliens, who Minnie had somehow missed and was rushing towards her. For some reason he looked like some sort of lame groundskeeper type person instead of a cool alien like the others.

Wait a minute – you're not imaginary, Minnie realised, pointing the flag at the man.

"Put that down!" the groundskeeper shouted.

Minnie pegged it over to the hole and jammed the flag back in. She did this so violently that the bottom of the hole gave way and the flag disappeared into it, as if under the little golf hole there was a much larger hole. Not expecting this, Minnie fell forwards, but turned it into a forward roll and came out of that in a run.

The groundskeeper didn't follow. The whole flag disappearing into the green thing had sucked the crossness out of him.

He looked at the hole for a moment, then decided to leave it. This was Beanotown. He'd lived here all his life. He knew by now it was best to leave weirdness alone, because if you poke weirdness, weirdness gets bigger.

ESSENTIAL WORKS

Resetting the router didn't work.

There was more shouting about what a harsh, unforgiving environment the house was for a 10-year-old boy without Wi-Fi.

Then, shouting from both parents about how when they were children Wi-Fi didn't exist, and how they'd had to do things in the real world, like climb trees and do jumps on a bike and generally be outside. Dennis loved all that stuff too, but there was now a thing he couldn't do (use Wi-Fi), so that was now all he could think about.

None of which helped Gnasher get back to sleep, or got Dennis any closer to making the Wi-Fi turn back on.

Suddenly Dad was stood behind Dennis, looking on his phone. "There's a site you can go on that tells you..." he started, before tailing off to read something on his screen. "Ah – there," he said proudly after a few moments. "Wi-Fi's off for half the town. Nothing we can do. Essential works."

He started to walk away, still reading the article, like the problem had been solved.

"BUT!" Dennis shouted after him.

"THE!" Dennis continued, leaving a nice big space in between his words to give them extra meaning. **"WI-FI'S... "**

"Says here someone messed up the internet with a giant magnet," Dad interrupted. "Caused a huge power surge that blew the system."

"Giant magnet?" Dennis asked. His recent activities had involved a giant magnet.

Dad read the website further. "Yeah. Someone got a huge magnet too near one of those green cupboard things on the street. That's where the wires and gubbins for the net are."

"So?"

"Magnets mess up electronics."

GRRRRR, Dennis thought, Walter broke the internet! It's definitely not half my fault. I'm not to blame in any way!

"They should just turn it off and on again," said Dad. "That always works."

Gnasher trotted downstairs to see what was going on. He'd given up on trying to sleep. It was like trying to doze off in the middle of the ring during a wrestling match.

"Wait!" Dennis said, realising something. He pointed at Dad's phone. "How come you can read the net then?"

Dad looked up and smiled. "I'm on mobile data," he announced.

"I need that to look at videos!" Dennis exclaimed. Dad stuffed his phone deep into his pocket.

"Use up all my data on videos? No way! Let's make a rocket."

Which was probably the only thing you could have said to Dennis at that moment to redirect their conversation.

Rocket?
"YES! Let's!"
Dennis agreed.

BOOOOF!

So Dad showed Dennis how to make a rocket.

First Dennis had to find the foot pump, which took a bit of time as it was lost in the garage. Then he had to find an empty plastic bottle. There weren't any in the recycling bin, so Dennis drank half a big bottle of sugar-free cola. (Rather than waste it.)

"BuUUuuuUUURP!"

Dennis burped in triumph once he'd downed the last drops.

Impressive, thought Gnasher.

"Now what?" Dennis asked Dad.

Dad was already raking around in the kitchen drawer. You know the one I'm talking about. The one that's full of random junk like watches, 3D cinema glasses, foreign plug adapters, ex-phones that haven't been charged for years. That drawer.

"AHA!" he shouted. "The vital ingredient!" He held up a small roll of black electrical tape.

Dennis asked what it was for, and Dad showed him how by wrapping tape round and round the valve of the foot pump, you could make it big enough to fit tightly into the neck of the pop bottle.

"The tighter the better," Dad said, jamming the fattened end of the valve into the top of the bottle. "There. Done!" he said, holding up the bottle-pump.

Dennis was disgusted. "That's not a rocket!"

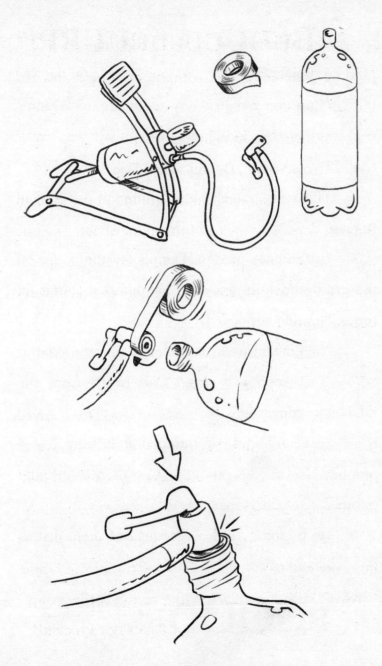

Gnasher had to agree. It just looked like a random thing.

"Can you not just buy me a drone?" Dennis suggested. "Other kids have loads of drones – why can't I?"

"Take it outside and pump it up," Dad suggested.

In the back garden, Dennis lay the bottle on the grass and pumped the foot pump a couple of times. Nothing happened.

"Is it meant to do something?" Dennis asked.

"Just keep pumping," Dad called from the kitchen window.

So Dennis did. He pumped and pumped and pumped. In fact, he pumped more than he usually pumped after Christmas dinner!

He pumped until his leg ached. Then, just as he was about to complain a bit more...

BOOOOF!

The bottle shot off the pump valve, whooshed across the garden and landed in a bush.

Dennis laughed. **"AWESOME!"**

"Very nice," commented Dad. "There is something you can do so it comes right back to you."

"Aw, cool! What?" asked Dennis. "Put special wings on it so it flies round in a circle?"

"Nope," said Dad. "You don't have to change the bottle at all."

Dennis thought for a moment before realising the answer.

What is the answer?
What can Dennis do that doesn't change the bottle, but will make it come back to him?

"Shoot it straight up!" Dennis said.

"Right," said Dad. "You'll need to stand it in a box for that. Also, if you fill it half full of water before jamming the valve in, it should go further."

Dennis ran to the recycling to find a box.

"You can bling the bottle up more with cardboard fins and stuff if you want, but don't do a lift-off in the garden. Knowing you, you'll smash a window. Or it'll land six gardens over. Do it in the park."

THE SAD KING OF ALL HE SURVEYED

Mayor Wilbur was sad. It was beginning to look like he'd never rule the world with an iron fist.

Things had gone well up until a few years ago when he'd risen, through some rather shady dealings, to the lofty position of Mayor. After that, the plan had been to become a member of parliament.

Then, probably through more shady dealings, he'd eventually become Prime Minister. He'd been hoping from there he would be a hop, skip and a jump away from becoming the ruler of the world.

But no. Somehow he'd got stuck here in this pokey little town, which was barely even on the map.

Was Beanotown even marked on the map? Wilbur thought suddenly.

He opened the bottom drawer of his desk. The one with loads of random junk like watches, 3D cinema glasses, foreign plug adapters, ex-phones that haven't been charged for years, etcetera. He rummaged around before pulling out a map of the UK. Opening it out on his desk and smoothing out the creases, he scoured the map from Land's End to John o' Groats.

"It's not even on the map!" he exclaimed loudly to himself, slapping the desk. No wonder satnavs never had a clue where to go in town.

Wilbur was getting tense. He pressed the button on his telephone-intercom thingy.

"Sandra, I'm off out for a few rounds of golf."

Golf always helped Wilbur relax. There was just something he enjoyed about hitting small defenceless things very hard with a stick.

Sandra (Dennis's mum) didn't answer. She wasn't there. It was Saturday. She was in the hall under a pile of wellies, wishing she had noise-cancelling headphones.

There must be some way of rising above it all, Wilbur thought as he went down to his car. But how?

Unbeknownst to him, Dennis – who had just run past, on the way to the park – was about to help him find a way to rise far, far above it all.

YEAH, BUT WHAT IS IT?

Dennis and Gnasher had found the bit in the middle of the park that was the furthest away from anything, in between the woods and the duck pond.

Dennis set the rocket up so it was pointing, pretty much, straight up. The bottle was half full of water from the tap at home. He could refill from the duck pond for the next go.

Dennis started pumping... and pumping... and pumping. This thing had a funny habit of going off the moment before you were ready to give up. With each pump the water in the bottle bubbled with the air that was being pumped into it.

Gnasher saw a familiar figure approach. Uh-oh, he thought. This won't end well.

"Whatcha doin'?" asked Minnie.

Dennis groaned. "What are you doing here?" he asked.

She was the last person he wanted to see

because Minnie had a sort of mutant superpower. She'd get carried away with things – often with imaginary ideas and situations. But, strangely, whenever she did, the people around her would get carried away too.

They'd become completely wrapped up in her made-up world, and before you knew it everyone in the supermarket, library, ice rink or wherever it was would start going bonkers. Her imagination and ideas seemed to be infectious.

The best way to deal with Minnie was not to get involved.

"The Wi-Fi's off in our house," Minnie told Dennis. "So, I dunno, I was gonna do something epic and retro like go on the zip line. Like in Roman times."

"Your mum kicked you out of the house?" Dennis guessed.

"It was Dad. He said I was sighing out of my nose too loudly."

Dennis knew better than to ask how you sigh out of your nose. He was still pumping the rocket, but was trying to act natural about it and really hoping Minnie wouldn't show any interest.

"What's that?" asked Minnie. "It looks interesting."

"This is a one-person-and-his-dog kinda thing."

"But what is it?" Minnie asked as Dennis pressed the pump one last time and...

BOOOOF!

The bottle shot off into the air on a jet of water, so fast and so high Dennis lost sight of it for a moment.

Minnie burst out laughing. **"AWESOME!"** she shouted.

Dennis caught sight of the rocket again. It was off course. It must have been leaning over slightly, or maybe there was a wind up there.

It was heading off towards the trees! If it landed in a tree he'd... well, he'd have to drink a load more sugar-free cola or something. (Luckily it wasn't heading the other way, towards the duck pond – if it landed on Duck Island, things would get complicated.)

"Me next!" Minnie said, as the bottle started rocketing back down. Dennis couldn't tell at first if

it was going to land in front of, or in, the trees. He started running towards it.

Gnasher decided (wrongly) that this was one of those fetch games and raced off to get the bottle first.

"Gnasher! No!" Dennis shouted, knowing that if Gnasher got a hold of the plastic bottle his gnashy gnashers would shred it in seconds.

Gnasher ignored Dennis as he sprinted off in the direction of the bottle.

Which landed in the trees.

Dennis started to groan, but have you ever tried to groan while running? It's not easy.

There was still a chance that the bottle wouldn't get stuck in a tree and that Gnasher wouldn't make a hole in it... It was a miniscule chance, but Dennis kept running. Closely followed by Minnie.

The vibe in Beanotown Woods was always a bit spooky. The trees grew too close together, and they seemed to have way too many leaves, blocking out the sun. So even in the middle of a lovely summer day – like it was – Beanotown Woods were in constant gloom.

Despite already having lost sight of the bottle, Dennis ran on. He continued in a straight line, hoping to rediscover it.

I'm hungry, thought Dennis. He'd grumpily not eaten much pasta the night before, to show Mum that she shouldn't have bothered fetching him. Dennis was regretting that now, but he had to ignore his stomach. He had a rocket to find.

Out in the park, the grass was pretty flat, but in the woods the forest floor was very different – awesome for mountain bikes and BMXs. Dennis slid down one little hill and clambered up another, grabbing hold of roots to help him.

Then he realised he hadn't seen Gnasher since he'd entered the woods. Where was his furry friend? He looked round, spotting Minnie following him.

"Have you seen..." Dennis started.

But Minnie disappeared.

And by that I don't mean she hid behind a tree or ducked down behind a bush. I mean, as Dennis looked at her, not too far away, Minnie was suddenly gone.

Had the same thing happened to Gnasher? Had he also disappeared?

Shocked, Dennis staggered back and...

f e l l

d

o

w

n

a

hole.

I BLAME DAD AND WI-FI FOR THIS!

Dennis was about to eat a cheese sandwich.

He didn't realise that it was odd to be suddenly home again, about to eat a cheese sandwich, but odder than that, as he brought the sandwich near his mouth, a big tongue came out from between the slices of bread and licked his face.

Dennis woke from his dream, at the bottom of a hole in the middle of the woods. Gnasher was licking his face.

"Get off, Gnasher!" Dennis spluttered, and pushed him away. Then he hugged his dog. "So this is where you went!"

Dennis got to his feet and tried to climb out through the gap above him, but the dirt was too loose and he couldn't get a proper hold on anything.

He looked up, out of the hole.

There it was.

The pop bottle was far above him, caught in the tree.

"I blame Dad and Wi-Fi for this!" Dennis said to Gnasher. "Him and his inventions."

Suddenly he remembered what he'd just seen. Minnie had disappeared! Hadn't she?

He'd been knocked out and had a dream about a sandwich licking his face. Had Minnie disappearing been a part of that dream? It had to be.

People don't just disappear in front of your eyes.

"**MINNIE!**" Dennis shouted up, out of the hole. "**MINNIE!**" he shouted again, but her familiar annoying face didn't come into view.

Dennis looked around for a root or something to pull himself up with. It was only then he realised he wasn't in a hole at all.

He was in a tunnel!

Dennis raised an eyebrow and turned to Gnasher. "Looks like we're in the Viking tunnels," he said.

Well duh! thought Gnasher.

Vikings were never tunnellers. But six or seven hundred years ago something weird had happened to a bunch of Vikings who landed on the small stretch of coast that would one day become Beanotown.

Shortly afterwards, they'd found a crystal skull. Looking at the skull for too long gave them headaches and strange ideas, and they started

doing very un-Viking things, like digging a network of tunnels and building strange steam- and clockwork-powered robots.

But none of that's got anything to do with this story. This is more a case of two different, unconnected stories lightly brushing up against each other.

The tunnel split off in two directions. There seemed to be a faint glow coming out of the darkness down one way, so Dennis went towards it.

"Hello," Dennis said to himself, when he reached the source of the light. It was one of the Viking robots, long since broken down hundreds of years ago.

"I'll call you Clanky," Dennis decided.

It lay in a heap on the floor. From the lack of pipes, Dennis presumed rightly that this was one of the clockwork type. In the middle of its chest was the source of the light, a dimly glowing blue disc. It was easily unscrewed and, upon its removal, Dennis saw that the glow was from a liquid inside the disc. Much like the liquid inside a glow stick – but better because this had lasted hundreds of years – shaking it made it glow a little brighter.

Using this to light the way, Dennis and Gnasher ventured further into the tunnels, hoping to find a way out.

Unnoticed by the boy and his dog, the ancient, seemingly long-dead robot moved slightly. You know, like things in horror films do.

As Dennis moved deeper and deeper into the tunnels, he was also unaware that he was travelling downwards as well. The slope was so slight that he was very surprised when he came to a huge underground cavern.

Set into the roof of the cavern was a giant jet engine. It wasn't the size you get on planes. It was the size you get on spacecraft!

"Woah, dude!" Dennis said.

Gnasher had to agree.

Now I know what you're thinking: this is silly. There is no way Vikings invented the jet engine. (This was actually a Victorian age jet engine, but you don't find that out just yet.)

But jet engine technology is a little older than you think. For the first jet engine you have to go back to the year 10. (That's right. I didn't leave any numbers off.) Back in the year 10, a thing called Hero's engine used jets of steam. That's more than 2000 years ago! But it wasn't until around the year 900 that jets really got going, with the invention of fireworks.

What I'm trying to say here is, you're wrong.

It's perfectly normal for a really old jet engine to be hidden in a cave under Beanotown.

Shining the light on its side, Dennis saw the letters BB marked on the engine in gold. He turned to Gnasher. "I think I know who built this," he said.

Gnasher gave Dennis his best "Whu?" look.

Over at Dennis's house, his mum opened the fridge door, took out the milk and sloshed what was left around in the bottle.

They were running low on milk!

... Which is quite a weird cliffhanger to end a chapter on.

BIG BUTT

Let's rewind to when Dennis was in the woods and had seen Minnie disappear.

From Dennis's point of view, she had done just that. Suddenly Minnie wasn't there.

From Minnie's point of view, something else happened.

Imagine you're watching TV, a programme set in a forest. Then imagine someone changes the channel to a science-fiction film. Instantly the trees you're looking at are replaced with something very different. Now imagine you're **inside** the TV when it happens.

There should have been a sound. There should have been a flash, or something, but there wasn't.

Suddenly Minnie was in the centre of a huge, brightly lit dome. She was standing on a lit circle, and in a ring above her were what looked like six massive lasers.

They were all pointing directly at her.

It was a teleporting machine! And it looked pretty serious.

In the forest, Dennis had been in front of her. Now the tallest woman Minnie had ever seen was standing in front of her.

The tallest *woman*? No. That wasn't right. This person may have had two eyes, a nose and a mouth on her face, in the same general arrangement as us humans do, but her face was purple. And she may have been breathing in through her nose but it looked a lot like this woman was breathing out through slits either side of her neck. Gills. Like. A. Fish.

It was obvious to Minnie what had happened.

She'd been abducted by aliens.

"Finally!" she said, with her fists firmly on her hips. "You took your time."

Compared to everyday life, alien abduction had often looked to Minnie like a better option.

Being in school? Rather be abducted by aliens.

Trudging around the supermarket? Rather be abducted by aliens.

Sitting through a wedding or a christening? Rather be abducted by aliens.

Minnie had often comforted herself with the thought that she could be abducted by aliens anywhere or at any time. There'd just be a light and maybe a **ZOOP!** noise, and suddenly she wouldn't be in whatever boring place it was anymore.

Minnie was a bit disappointed that there hadn't been a light and a ZOOP! She'd have to talk to the alien science boffins about fixing that.

There did seem to be a couple of science-boffin creatures next to the boss lady. (The tall purple alien was clearly the boss.) They were much shorter – shorter than Minnie – and grey and weird and ugly. They also had what looked like thick welding goggles on.

Behind the boffins was the muscle. A third alien species. These were almost as tall as the alien boss lady, but much wider and cross-looking. They all looked like they'd been working out. They were also holding what had to be laser – or maybe plasma – blasters.

Minnie thought, I need to get me one of those.

Alien boss lady seemed surprised by Minnie saying, "Finally! You took your time!" She turned to one of the little grey science aliens and said, "Is the translator working properly? Did she really just say that?"

The creature checked the translating computer in front of him (or her, it was hard to tell). "Er... everything seems to be in working order, your excellency."

Her excellency turned her attention back to Minnie. "You are a prisoner of the BigButt Alliance!"

Minnie laughed in her face.

The alien boss turned back to the science creature at the translator screen. "Why's she laughing?" she asked.

"You said 'butt'!" Minnie told her.

The alien boss lady didn't get it.

And to know why she didn't get it, you need to know how the translator works...

Noise-cancelling headphones work by creating a noise that is opposite to the sound outside your earphones. So if someone coughs, noise-cancelling headphones create a noise that is the opposite of a cough. Together, the two sounds cancel each other out and you can't hear anything.

The alien translator works similarly, replacing other languages with your own. The translator sends the translation directly to your ear along a narrow, invisible infrared beam. Meaning that you only hear your translation and not anybody else's.

But the translator messes up sometimes when someone says a word in one language that doesn't exist in another. It uses a random word that sounds sort of close. So while the alien boss lady was saying a perfectly acceptable word in her own language, Minnie was hearing "BigButt".

The alien boss turned back to Minnie and restarted. "You are a prisoner of the BigButt Alliance!"

Minnie smirked.

"I am Lady BigButt. You are to—"

Before Lady BigButt could finish, Minnie started laughing again.

Lady BigButt was suddenly furious, turning a darker shade of purple. She pushed the toad-like science creature out of the way.

"Let's have a look at that!" she said.

She studied the screen.

"Here we go..."

She tapped the translator screen a few times, moved a few things around, then spoke again.

"I am Lady BigBad. You are a prisoner of the BigBad Alliance!"

She'd tinkered with the translation – Minnie wasn't impressed.

Lady BigBad continued, "You will now spend your days in the battle arena!"

"Cool!" said Minnie.

Lady BigBad turned to the science creature again. "Are you sure the translator's working properly, Splerch?"

Splerch couldn't think what to do. As far as he could tell, the translator was working perfectly. But he could also tell that Lady BigBad was moments away from sending *him* to the battle arena too. Nervously sweating, he turned to Lady BigBad, shrugged, and smiled weakly.

Creatures like him didn't do well in the battle arena.

PROJECT ICARUS

"Cool!" said Dennis, back on Earth. Or, rather, under it.

What's this giant jet engine here for though? Dennis wondered. Then he realised...

This was Project Icarus!

Not too long ago, Dennis and Gnasher had found themselves on Duck Island, a lazily named island in the middle of Beanotown duck pond. In Victorian times, one of the founders

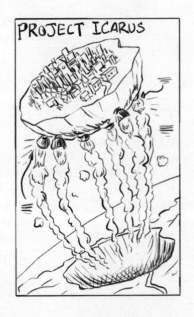

of the town, Barry Beano, had discovered the dinosaurs that lived there and had tried to build a dinosaur park. This had gone terribly wrong.

Because... dinosaurs.

73

But at one point in that adventure, Dennis and Gnasher had found themselves in Barry Beano's old design office and had read about Project Icarus. It was a plan to make the town fly!

Dennis had assumed at the time (because Beanotown isn't flying) that perhaps Barry had realised, or been told, that it was a stupid, dangerous idea and he'd thought better of it.

Obviously Dennis was wrong. There was at least one enormous jet under the town. Probably many more.

Dennis smiled at Gnasher, who smiled back. "It'd be pretty cool to live in a flying town," he said.

Gnasher had to agree.

Dennis stood with his fists on his hips in triumph. But the good feeling quickly evaporated.

There was a large, important-looking button near the jet. Grinning, Dennis thought about pressing it, but before he did, he remembered the time he'd pressed the "Release Zombie Gas" button at Beanotown's top-secret research station.

His grin slipped a little.

There had also been the time he pressed the button at Horrible Hall marked, "Don't press this button or the headless headmaster of Horrible Hall will be released".

Dennis's grin turned to a worried smile.

And how about the time he was in the school kitchen and pressed the "Get hit in the face by a custard pie" button?

"What do we do now?" Dennis asked Gnasher, not grinning at all anymore.

Gnasher gave him his best "Pop to the butchers and buy me some sausages?" look.

But what they both quickly decided to do next was run.

The old rusty robot, Clanky, burst in, headed straight for Dennis and Gnasher!

Ka-lunk ka-lunk ka-lunk...

SWOOSH! went Clanky's metal fingers

through the air as it made a grab for them. Dennis dodged out of the way just in time, as Gnasher leapt over it. (Normally Gnasher couldn't jump that high. You need to be avoiding ancient robots or monsters or something for that kind of height.)

They ran across the cavern and into the tunnel on the other side, Clanky's clanky feet **ka-lunk ka-lunk ka-lunking** after them. For a frightening moment, Gnasher thought he heard the ka-lunking in front of them too. Another robot?! But it was just an echo.

A few minutes later, the tunnel opened up into another large cave, also filled with a huge jet engine. Dennis and Gnasher didn't slow to admire it, though, as the robot behind them continued its pursuit.

They ran across the cavern and into the tunnel on the far side. If the jets are in place to make Beanotown fly, this tunnel probably forms a ring around the town, Dennis thought. He didn't say it, because he was starting to get tired and out of breath.

Dennis spotted a small glimmer of light in the roof of the tunnel ahead. He threw the light disc at Clanky, shouting "Catch!".

For a moment, Gnasher ran after the disc, his fetch instinct kicking in. But quickly enough he thought, Woah! What am I doing?!

Dennis ran towards the small hole in the ceiling, as Gnasher caught up.

The hole above them wasn't big enough to escape through.

It was tiny. About the width of a coaster. Maybe his arm could escape, but not the rest of him. It was also on the roof of the tunnel. Even Dennis's best jump wouldn't be quite high enough. He could see sky through the hole, though. So near and yet so far!

Then a hard-boiled egg came flying down through the hole and hit Dennis on the forehead. He staggered back. A hard-boiled egg?!

Next, a hand came down through the hole, followed by the arm it was attached to. Someone was saving them from Clanky!

Dennis looked round for the robot, but it wasn't there. Had Clanky only wanted his tummy light back?

Dennis ran forwards, jumped, and grabbed

the helpful hand, yanking the rest of the arm down through the hole. As Dennis noticed a small flag pole lying on the floor of the tunnel, whoever was on the other end of the arm screamed in terror. Bits of dirt and the tunnel ceiling rained down, making the hole bigger. Quite suddenly there was a mini cave-in, the hole widened, and a familiar head appeared.

SOME BWARPS?

Meanwhile, in space, Minnie was being taken to the battle arena. She was a huge fan of American wrestling, so was quite excited by the prospect, though she was trying to act cool.

Minnie was in the back of a hover van. Lady BigBad wasn't there. She was off doing evil alien leader stuff. Minnie went over to the barred window into the driver's cabin.

"What's my theme tune?" Minnie asked the driver.

The driver didn't understand the question.

"What?" he said, barely looking round.

"My theme tune," Minnie repeated. "I need entrance music to come out to. Something rocky. Heavy guitars. Maybe some dubstep BWARPs?"

The driver didn't have a clue what she was talking about (and neither do I).

"I also need a name. Minnie's not a fighter

name." She thought for a moment. "Or is it? Maybe I could use it... The Minnie Tornado? The Minnie Destroyer? Hmm, it needs work. On the posters I want fire and explosions behind me and my name in, like, a metal font. Like the words are made out of steel!"

The driver was deeply confused. He didn't understand what this human was saying, even though the translator in the van was transmitting all the words into his ears perfectly. They just didn't seem to be arranged in an order that made any sense.

On top of that, this prisoner wasn't acting like a prisoner. Normally they'd scream and cry at the prospect of being taken to the battle arena, what with the certain injury and all. This human was acting like she was someone rich and famous and he was her driver or agent. Had he missed something? Was she not a prisoner?

Giving up, Minnie looked out of the window. They were driving along a road. Above, Minnie could see space. The things they were whizzing past looked like buildings. Everything had a city-of-the-future vibe. Not a spaceship vibe. How far away from Earth was she? Could a teleport do-hicky teleport you to a different planet?

She went back to the driver's window.

"Hey! Buddy! Are we on a planet or a spaceship? Because it's not obvious."

Finally! thought the driver. A question that made sense.

"We're on the BigBad Alliance's city ship," he answered.

Cool, thought Minnie. So it's both. A city and a ship! Nice.

On the road ahead, Minnie saw a large structure looming. It looked like one of the cooler, more designery football stadiums back on Earth.

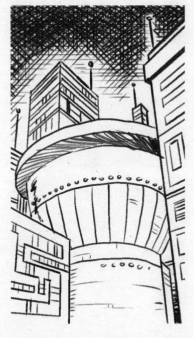

Back on Earth? Minnie liked the sound of that. Back on Earth. She'd have to work that into conversation later. Back on Earth, we do this. Back on Earth, we do that. Yeah, that sounded good.

The stadium was obviously this battle arena she was meant to be going to. She sat back down, then suddenly realised something and rushed back to the driver's window.

"**Wait!** We've forgotten something!" she shouted, sounding slightly panicky.

This is more like it, thought the driver. The pleading. The crying. The protests that this is all some big mistake. Here we go...

"I need an outfit!" Minnie said. "Something metallic, with maybe a lightning bolt on it. I can't fight in this!"

Nope, thought the driver, as the van zipped in through the large gates to the arena. We're back to confusing again.

DETENTION UNTIL YOUR LATE FORTIES

A little earlier, back on Earth – she's right, that *does* sound good – Mayor Wilbur strode out onto the fourth green. If you recall, he'd gone golfing to clear his head and cheer himself up.

The first three holes had gone well. He'd hit the tiny, defenceless ball very hard. It had gone near enough to the holes to be knocked in with just two or three more knocks. Wilbur was starting to feel better.

He came to the fourth green. It didn't register that the flag normally poking out of the hole wasn't there. He lined up his shot and took it. The ball rolled towards the hole and plonked down.

So far, so normal.

Mayor Wilbur walked over to the hole, put his hand in to retrieve the ball – and another hand, under the ground, grabbed it!

That was the moment where things stopped being normal. The hand pulled the rest of his arm into the hole, and kept on pulling! The only thing that stopped him was the side of his face getting slammed into the perfectly mowed grass.

The unseen underground hand continued to pull and Mayor Wilbur became aware of someone screaming. It was him!

The patch of grass his face was pressed

against gave way slightly, and the Mayor realised he may have started screaming a little early. Now was the time to start screaming. Then the ground under his face gave way and his head was pulled underground.

Quickly becoming accustomed to the subterranean gloom, Wilbur saw... Dennis!

The Mayor couldn't believe it! He was used to Dennis's prank-playing. He was familiar with the boy's whoopee cushions and other similarly annoying devices – but this was on a whole other level!

To set this up, Dennis must have dug some sort of tunnel that led directly under the hole in the green. How had he known when the Mayor was going to be there? He, himself had only just decided! (Dennis, as we know, knew nothing.)

The roof of the tunnel properly caved in then, and Wilbur fell in, closely followed by his golf clubs. (It was only then that Dennis realised the hard-boiled egg must have actually been a golf ball!)

Earlier, Minnie had jammed the flag into the hole on the golf green so hard it'd broken through the ceiling of the tunnel underneath.

Wilbur lay on the tunnel floor feeling slightly dazed, covered in dirt. Gnasher said hello by licking his face.

Wilbur spluttered and pushed Gnasher away.

"You've gone too far this time, Dennis!" he shouted, as more dirt fell on him. "I'll have you..." He faltered. Wilbur was having trouble thinking of what could be done. The boy was 10. "I'll have you put in detention until your late forties!" he finally said.

"What did I do?!" protested the boy, looking very hard done by.

"You've just pulled me through a small hole in the ground, for one!" Mayor Wilbur pointed out. "Then there's digging a tunnel without planning permission. How did you do that by the way?" he asked. "Aren't you meant to go to school?!"

The Mayor looked down both directions of the tunnel. It was much larger and longer than required for this elaborate prank. It must have taken the boy months.

"I didn't dig the tunnels," Dennis told the Mayor. "I just fell down here and was trying to get out!"

For once, Wilbur believed him.

"Tunnels? What for?" asked the filthy, high-ranking town official.

"I dunno." Dennis shrugged. "It seems like it's just a way to get to the jet engines."

"Jet engines?" asked the grubby leader, suddenly intrigued.

BORF AND BLERCH

The van with Minnie inside arrived at the battle arena.

Borf and Blerch both smiled at each other. It was always fun when someone new was brought to the arena. The crying. The pleading innocence. The begging to be let go. The appeals to their better nature... They were the most fun, because Borf and Blerch had been chosen for that job because of their complete lack of a better nature.

So when Minnie sprung out of the van with a huge smile on her face, eager to make a start, they were every bit as confused as the hover-van driver had been, and really disappointed.

"Are you going to show me where I need to be?" Minnie asked impatiently.

Normally it was a case of dragging the terrified arrival to the cells while it pleaded with them and tried to explain what a terrible, awful mistake was

being made. This time, however, Borf and Blerch had to march quicker to catch up with Minnie, who was striding ahead saying things like, "This way, is it?"

They glanced at each other. Something wasn't quite right. Was this thing a prisoner or not?

They were in one of the many corridors behind the seating of the main arena. As they passed a window down to the arena floor, the crowd of fifty thousand or more aliens cheered the arrival of two more contenders. Minnie rushed to the window to watch the battle.

"Lift me up!" she said to Borf. "I can't see!"

Borf found himself doing just that.

Minnie peered down into the arena. If gorillas were 11-foot-tall blue lizards with horns, they'd look like the first contender. And if raspberry jelly had a bunch of eyes in it, that's what contender number two would look like.

Minnie watched eagerly as the blue lizardy thing stepped forwards. The raspberry jelly formed

a mouth out of its gelatinous mass and screamed.
The lizard made a fist and brought it down hard on
the jelly creature.

SPLAT!

The match was over.

The crowd went wild. The aliens with feet
stood up and cheered.

Minnie was disgusted. She was used to
wrestling.

"Put me down! Put me down!" she said to
Borf. **"What was that?!"** she complained, as the
raspberry jelly tried to pull itself back together.

"So the monkey lizard's the bad guy, right?"
she continued. "Where was the taunting of the
crowd? And I'm not one of those losers who thinks
the baddie should always lose, but whoever loses
has to look like they're gonna win near the end,
right before they lose! Where's the drama?!"

Borf and Blerch looked at each other. They

didn't have a clue what she was on about. And more confusing still, Minnie wasn't talking to them like a prisoner. She was talking to them like a boss. Had they missed something?

Down in the arena, the raspberry jelly was having trouble squelching away because the lizard thing had pounded it so hard that a bit of it was stuck to the arena floor. A small three-legged alien rushed out with a huge spatula and started to scrape the jelly alien off the arena floor, like an egg that had stuck to the frying pan.

For the first time since Minnie had been told she was to be put in the battle arena, she was worried. Terrified, even. Terrified that she was going to be in something totally lame!

NOT REALLY RULES,
BUT GUIDELINES

In an odd way to start a chapter, Dennis's mum found Dennis's dad in the living room reading one of his classic comics and told him they were low on milk and out of bread. Dennis's dad knew that being told they were low on milk and out of bread was the same as being told to go to the shop to get some milk and bread.

"I'll go get some, shall I?" he suggested.

Not far away, Dennis and Gnasher were showing Mayor Wilbur one of the jets under Beanotown. Using the light from his phone, Wilbur stared at it in wonder.

"I think there's, like, a ring of them round the town," Dennis said, as if a ring of buried jets under a town was a normal thing.

"Why?" asked the Mayor.

Dennis shrugged. "It's probably Project Icarus."

"What's Project Icarus?" Wilbur asked.

So Dennis told him about Barry Beano and his plan to make Beanotown fly. All the while the Mayor's eyes widened and an evil smile slowly grew across his face.

"I've heard quite a lot about Barry Beano," the Mayor said, more to himself than to Dennis. "He's got quite a file back at the town hall. I thought the dinosaur park was his biggest creation. I had no idea about this! I could activate these! I could make the town fly!"

"Cool!" said Dennis.

"Eh?" said the Mayor. "Really?"

There are rules to stories. Well... not really rules, but guidelines. It helps to have a hero or two. For them to be a hero they need something to do. So you need a baddie. For the whole hero–baddie story-system to work, baddies have to do something bad and the hero (or heroes) have to stop them.

At the minute, though, baddie number one

(Wilbur) is going to try to make the town fly, and hero number one (Dennis) thinks that's cool. And baddie number two (Lady BigBad) is putting Minnie in the battle arena, and hero number two (Minnie) also thinks that's cool.

So from a writing-a-story point of view it's not going well at all!

"Do you know the story of Icarus?" the Mayor asked Dennis. Dennis didn't. "Of course you don't. What do they teach you at that school?!"

"I dunno," Dennis said. "Mostly, I'm not listening."

Mayor Wilbur studied the jets in closer detail while he told Dennis of the legend of Icarus. "In Greek myth, King Minos hired a man called Daedalus to build a labyrinth, a huge maze, to keep the Minotaur, a half-man half-bull monster, trapped. But King Minos wanted it kept a secret, so he double crossed Daedalus and locked him and his son Icarus in a tower. Daedalus and Icarus managed to pinch enough feathers off seagulls to build wings – glued together with wax – to fly away, but when they did, Icarus flew too near the sun. The wax melted. Icarus's feathers fell off and he tumbled into the sea."

There was silence. Mayor Wilbur turned round. Dennis was crouching in front of Gnasher with his hands behind his back.

"Which hand is the fishy biscuit in, Gnasher?" he asked. "Which hand? Which hand?" he repeated, winding up Gnasher. Gnasher went snuffling from one hand to the other, then dived on Dennis, who fell over.

Dennis laughed, then realised everything had gone quiet. He turned to the Mayor. "Did you say something?"

"You didn't hear a word of what I just said, did you?" asked Wilbur.

"Yeah I did," Dennis said. "There was a king who had a cow in a maze then, er... seagulls, or something? Great story. Can't wait for the film."

"Never mind. I will elevate this town. The only way from here is up... I need to get the boffins at the top-secret research station to test these jets first."

Wilbur strode off, back to the golf course hole, pulling his phone out of his pocket as he did so.

"They can bring a ladder too."

Dennis followed him. "And I need to tell Minnie! She'll think this is awesome!" Then Dennis stopped and remembered Minnie's disappearance. Had it really happened? The only way to know for sure would be to find her.

The top-secret research station is really near the golf course, so the boffins didn't take long to get there. Dennis and Wilbur were soon up and out onto the golf course.

While Wilbur made some phone calls, Dennis and Gnasher ran off to the last place he'd seen Minnie: the woods.

And, across town... Wait for it... big cliffhanger coming up... Dennis's dad popped to the shops.

THE RASPBERRY
JELLY COUGHED

Minnie wasn't in the woods. She was in a room (or was it a cell?) off the corridor, backstage in the battle arena. Borf and Blerch tried to shove her in but she strode in so quickly their hands didn't touch her.

"Wait here till you're called!" Blerch said, trying to keep up his tough exterior. The truth was, though, that Minnie worried him.

She was small. The big aliens, the ones that wouldn't get instantly smushed, didn't fear the arena. But the small aliens who ended up in the battle arena were always scared. And rightly so, because they got smushed, and getting smushed really hurts.

This small alien wasn't at all scared, which made Blerch think maybe it knew something they didn't. Perhaps this "Minnie" had a secret power? Maybe lasers shot out of her eyes or something...

As Borf and Blerch slammed the door shut behind her, Minnie found herself in a large room with a lot of strange-looking aliens of all shapes and sizes.

A hush fell over the group. Everyone – big, scary aliens included – had seen her stride in briskly, in a really "not a prisoner" way. They all stared at her.

The door behind Minnie opened again and the two aliens who'd been fighting earlier entered. Well, one entered. The other was pushed into the room in a giant dish.

The raspberry jelly coughed. "I'll be alright," it said in a trembly voice.

At first Minnie was sad and concerned for the jelly creature.

"You okay, buddy?" she asked. One, then two, then a few more of the creature's eyes turned to Minnie.

"I just need a lie-down," it replied, but by this time Minnie was just staring into the jelly thing.

"You're trying to count my eyes, aren't you?" said Flurrnt (for that was its name).

"Who, me? No," said Minnie, as she tried to count its eyes.

The lizard-gorilla that had beaten the jelly walked over to one of the other big aliens. They high-fived and laughed evilly.

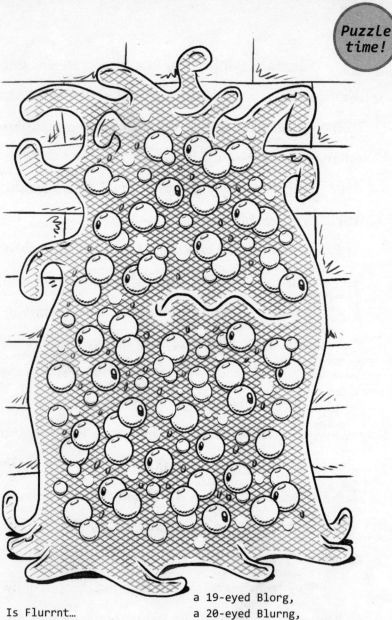

Is Flurrnt…
an 18-eyed Blant,

a 19-eyed Blorg,
a 20-eyed Blurng,
or a 21-eyed Hort?

And how many eyes are looking right? (Hint: Make sure you only count the eye balls and not the bubbles.)

On one wall there was a large video screen showing a live feed of the battle arena. Now, in the arena, there was what looked like a huge woodlouse (if woodlice stood up) facing a five-legged octopus-type thing. The woodlouse jumped. The octopus tried to run, but wasn't quick enough and the woodlouse landed on it, squashing it. The fight was over, already, and the crowd went wild, as the octopus-type thing squidged back.

The larger, meaner aliens in the room watched Minnie with interest. This was usually when the little ones freaked out.

Minnie turned from the screen and addressed the room. **"YOU CALL THIS ENTERTAINMENT?!"** she shouted. Everyone was surprised. "You're doing it all wrong!" Then everyone was confused.

"We need to work out some moves," Minnie announced. "You. Big guy. What's your name?" she said, pointing at something that looked like a cross between a pug dog and a dinosaur.

"Kurg," said Kurg.

"Come here, Kurg. Let me show you something."

The general vibe in the room was "What's going on?" This new red-and-black striped creature seemed to think it was in charge. Was it?

The dino-dog got up and walked over to Minnie. It was easily twice her size.

"Okay, you're big – that makes me the underdog. Even though you're the one who looks like a dog," Minnie started explaining. "That means people are gonna want to root for me. I don't need to win. I probably shouldn't until the end of the season, but it needs to look like I could win. Stand near that wall," she instructed the alien.

Without thinking, the alien did what it was told.

"Keep your legs apart. I'm going to slide through," explained Minnie.

The alien did as it was told, still not quite getting what was happening.

Minnie ran towards Kurg, then dropped and slid between the creature's legs. Behind it, she jumped up, bounced off the wall and jumped on Kurg's back.

There were a couple of "Oohs" and "Ahhs"

from the small audience of fellow fighters.

Minnie quickly scrambled up to the top of the thing and grabbed its ears. "Does this hurt?" she asked.

"No," Kurg answered.

"You need to act like it does," Minnie explained. "Cry out and stagger back so I'm squashed between you and the wall, but don't properly squash me."

The creature did as it was told, screaming out in fake, Oscar-winning agony, then staggering dramatically back.

When Minnie's back touched the wall, she acted like she was being crushed and let go of Kurg's ears. The alien stepped forwards and Minnie fell to the ground. She got up and dusted herself off.

"Well, it's a start I guess. Needs work."

One of the small aliens put one of its many hands up.

Minnie pointed to it. "Yes, you?"

"What if when Kurg steps forwards, instead

of falling to the ground, you lean your back to the wall and push off with your legs?"

"Yeah, then Kurg could fall over and you jump on him," suggested another small alien who was catching on.

Kurg was catching on too. "I didn't really buy the bit where you slid through my legs. I should try to grab you, but, you know, miss."

Minnie snapped her fingers and pointed at the alien. "Nice! **I love it!** Let's try that again, from the top."

THE CHORUS OF CAR ALARMS

It didn't take Dennis and Gnasher long to get to the woods.

"Where's Minnie?" Dennis urged Gnasher. "Go on, sniff her out! There's a good boy!"

Gnasher lowered his nose, sniffed the earth and set off looking for Minnie's scent. It wasn't long before he found it and rushed off deeper into the woods, Dennis following closely behind.

Eventually Gnasher stopped, because Minnie's trail stopped.

This was weird to Gnasher. Trails never just stop. You can't just suddenly stop having a scent – but it seemed like that was just what Minnie had done!

Gnasher gave Dennis his best "Huh?" look.

"What is it, boy?" Dennis asked. "Which way now?"

Gnasher gave Dennis his best "I dunno" look.

Dennis took in the rest of his environment. This was it. They were back where Minnie had been standing when she'd disappeared. So she HAD disappeared! It wasn't a dream!

What do I do now? Dennis asked himself. How do I tell people Minnie suddenly disappeared and make them believe me?

Suddenly that worry was shoved to one side. Dennis heard it first. A low rumble that quickly got louder and louder.

Every bird in every tree all around them suddenly decided to take to the air at the same time. Then the ground shook and didn't stop shaking.

Dennis fell over. Gnasher didn't. Having a leg at each corner made him much more stable. All around them, leaves and bits of bark fell from the equally shaken trees. Not too far from them a tree fell over, with a huge **CRASH!**

Dennis and Gnasher's eyes darted back and

forth, looking out for the next tree to fall. Further away this time, another one did just that.

"What's going on?" Dennis asked Gnasher, who already had his best "I dunno" face ready from before.

Then the rumble faded and the ground slowly stopped shaking.

Phew, thought Dennis and Gnasher together. Thankfully, whatever it was was over now. (It wasn't over.)

They both ran from the woods to see how badly the rest of the town had been affected. Soon they cleared the tree line and ran out into the park.

Dennis and Gnasher saw how low the sun was getting. As usual they'd obviously lost track of time and it was later than they'd thought. From where they were it didn't look like any of the buildings had fallen. The only clue that anything weird had just happened was the chorus of car alarms that were going off throughout the town.

Then Dennis noticed that the sun was going down much faster than it did usually. The shadows from the trees were getting longer and moving across the grass. It was like watching a film on fast forward. Dennis looked down to his and Gnasher's shadows. He could see them moving too.

Then he realised. The sun wasn't going down. The town was going up!

A VERY SHORT CHAPTER

I always liked super-short chapters when I was a kid. I'd read them and announce proudly to my parents that I'd read a whole chapter already, keeping quiet about its length... Well, anyway...

Most people are like Dennis, if something weird is happening they think, What's happening? But there are some people who think, What's happening, and how can I turn this to my advantage?

Not far from Dennis, the Mayor's son Walter had felt the Earth shake and looked out of his bedroom window. He saw the sky move and thought, What's happening, and how can I turn this to my advantage?

THE BLEETABLOBS OF ZIGGABOB FIVE

Up in space, on board the BigBad Alliance's city ship, Lady BigBad was sitting on a throne in the executive box. The best seat in the whole of the battle arena. She'd come to see Minnie's first, and possibly last, battle.

She was going to watch it with interest, as Minnie hadn't been teleported here just for entertainment. The BigBad Alliance had existed for more than a thousand years through constant expansion. It was so big and needed so much food and fuel to keep it going. As a result, it relied on invading new planets to pinch all their food and drain all their water. The problem was, the more planets the Alliance invaded, the bigger, and hungrier, it grew.

A human had been picked to fight in the arena, to see how tough human beings were. Judging by her small size, invading and then taking over the Earth would be an easy task – but you could never be too sure. Sometimes strange aliens could surprise you. Like the Bleetablobs of Ziggabob Five who can fire laser beams out of their eyes.

Soon Lady BigBad would know everything she needed to: how strong and quick and clever humans were, and what the best and quickest way to defeat them would be. Would the robot shock-troops be best? They usually were. Or what about the Gurrak army? She hadn't used them in a while. Or the Zurp of Plurp? That was always fun.

... And, of course, Lady BigBad really liked watching the fighting. She may have been the regional leader of this particular spiral arm of the galaxy, but that didn't mean she couldn't have fun watching lesser beings hurt each other.

Down on the arena floor, the human called Minnie strode out, waving to the crowd. She was closely followed by Kurg, who snarled at the crowd and shook his fist.

Minnie and Kurg faced each other. A hush fell over the crowd, and something unexpected happened. The little alien (Minnie) ran at the big alien.

What was she going to do? Kurg was huge!

Kurg stepped forwards and at the last moment, Minnie dropped and slid between Kurg's legs. Kurg tried to grab her but she was sliding too quickly.

Behind Kurg, Minnie jumped up and free-ran at the wall, bouncing off it and jumping onto Kurg's back. She clambered up it, grabbed his ears and pulled.

Kurg cried out in pain and staggered back, squashing Minnie against the wall. Minnie let go of Kurg's ears and Kurg stepped forwards. With the wall at her back, Minnie pushed Kurg with her legs and Kurg fell on his face as Minnie dropped to the ground. Minnie dived onto Kurg, but before she landed, Kurg rolled over and Minnie landed harmlessly on the arena floor.

Lady BigBad and the fifty thousand other aliens couldn't believe their eyes! The battles were usually extremely short and horribly one sided, often consisting of one BOSH then the boshed one getting dragged out. Up till now that had been more than enough. Everyone had been entertained. Or thought themselves entertained. But if I'd grown up only eating sprouts I wouldn't have thought sprouts were bad, until I'd tried cake. Minnie and Kurg's fight was like a massive chocolate cake jammed into the mouths of a population that had only ever eaten over-cooked sprouts.

Minnie and Kurg both scrambled back to their feet and began to circle each other. Seemingly they were weighing each other up.

Then they went for it again. This small human was fearless! But why?

The crowd were on the edge of their seats.

It looked like Kurg now had the upper hand. He looked sure to win, but at the last moment, Minnie seemed to get some extra energy from somewhere and fought back.

Now it looked like Minnie was going to win! The crowd were on their feet. Then, just when it looked like Minnie had Kurg where she wanted him, Kurg dodged and turned the tables on the small alien.

Time and again, who was winning flipped from Minnie to Kurg and back to Minnie again. The crowd seemed split. Half were cheering for Kurg, half for Minnie.

Then finally, Minnie collapsed and, with her unable to fight, Kurg won, but only just.

Lady BigBad was speechless, and a little worried. She'd have to study this species more closely.

Down in the arena, Kurg held his fist high in

the air in triumph. The crowd erupted like it never had before.

Minnie struggled to her feet and Kurg took her hand, lifting it too. The crowd took it to another, higher level. They cheered and whooped and hollered, and threw... fruit?

Well it looked like fruit to Minnie. Kurg quickly picked up the odd assortment of offerings, but Minnie didn't take any. She didn't trust space fruit.

Kurg looked at her strangely. "Do you not want any of this money?" he asked.

"Money?!" Minnie said, picking up the last three fruits. "How much is this?" she asked, holding up a Bink, a Troob and a Flent.

Lady BigBad looked all around her at the cheering crowd.

Minnie and Kurg waved, and as they both staggered back through the doors to the arena floor the crowd didn't stop cheering.

$$🍓 + 🍓 + 🍓 = 30$$

$$🍓 + 🪵 + 🪵 = 20$$

$$🪵 + 🪵 + 🐛 = 12$$

$$🐛 + 🍓 + 🪵 = ?$$

Three Troobs are worth £30
A Troob and two Flents are worth £20
Two Flents and a Bink are worth £12
So how much is a Bink, a Troob and a Flent?

122

Lady BigBad turned to Ploop.

"Delay the invasion," she told him.

Delay the invasion? thought Ploop. How do I do that?!

Once backstage, the seemingly badly injured Minnie and Kurg stood straight again.

Kurg laughed. "Listen to them!" he said. "In all my battles I've never heard them cheer like that!"

A RIGHT STATE

It was all kicking off back at the golf course when Dennis and Gnasher got there. Scientist types from the top-secret research station were running around in panic mode. The Mayor was shouting at anyone and everyone, and half the golf course itself was missing. Well, not missing. Left behind.

"What are you doing?" Dennis yelled at the Mayor. "You just turned on all the jets straight away?! That's like something I'd do! Aren't grown-ups meant to think about stuff first?"

"We didn't do it on purpose!" the Mayor barked back. "I told the scientists to test the jets first. This is their fault!" he said, pointing at a random scientist. Then he shouted at them: **"THIS IS NOT WHAT I'D CALL A TEST!"**

They must have pressed the button Dennis had resisted pressing earlier!

"There's no OFF switch!" the Mayor

continued. "Only an idiot would press an on switch without first checking there was an off switch..."

The scientist he'd been pointing at started running around in circles and waving his hands in the air.

Earlier, Dennis had thought the idea of living in a flying town was cool, but now the scene had a general disaster movie vibe. Only not a very good one. Normal, proper disaster movies have a bit where scientists warn politicians about a potential disaster. In the films, the politicians ignore the scientists and then the disaster happens. In this case, the scientists had cut to the chase by creating the disaster themselves (with a little gentle persuasion from the Mayor, of course).

Project Icarus was in full swing!

Cautiously, Dennis moved towards the new edge that had appeared. Quickly getting freaked out by the realisation of what lay beyond it, and the growing wind, Dennis lay down and crawled on his belly until he could see over.

A lot of Beanotown was being left behind. Only the middle bit was rising into the air. The town had grown somewhat since Barry Beano had the ring of jets installed, in Victorian times. Most of the extra stuff that had been built later was still on the Earth. Mostly, it looked like what people called the "old town" was flying (the bit he was on), leaving a huge crater in the middle of Beanotown.

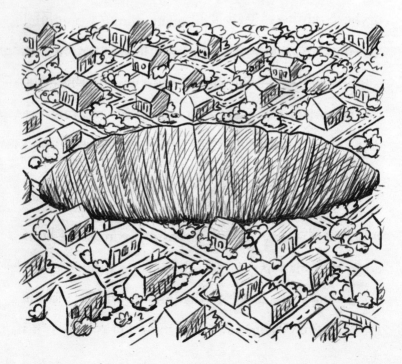

As the middle of town rose further into the sky, rotating as it did, Dennis looked for his house. It'd been built in the seventies. It wasn't one of the nice-looking expensive houses but it was pretty near "the posh bit".

Far below him, Dennis spotted the abandoned house at the end of his street. The one with the jungle garden and the broken roof. That was there, but the rest of his street wasn't. That meant his street was up here on the flying bit!

Dennis moved back, away from the edge. He didn't know what to feel about that. Was it a good or bad thing?

Dennis's parents thought it was a bad thing.

Minutes earlier, Dennis's dad had been in the mini supermarket. They were low on milk and out of bread. He went round, got the milk and bread. Plus some sliced cheese. A chocolate bar. Some brown sauce. Some sausages for Gnasher... and found himself at the self-service till without a bag.

Refusing to buy a bag, he stuffed his pockets with cheese and brown sauce, and carried the rest in his arms. As he approached the end of his street, by the abandoned house, the ground beneath his feet shook.

An earthquake? In Beanotown?

He staggered back as a crack opened up in the pavement in front of him, then quickly spread across the road.

With a bump, the ground on the other side of the crack jumped up. Then Dennis's dad watched in horror as the ground in front of him continued to rise.

"NO! WAIT!" he yelled.

He quickly ran forwards and threw the milk and bread up onto the path in front of him. He jammed the chocolate bar in his mouth, then leapt and grabbed the pavement as the ground he was on continued to fall.

Awkwardly he just managed to clamber up to safety. As he pulled himself onto the pavement, the plastic brown sauce bottle burst and squirted brown-ness up his shirt. He was a right state, but at least he was safe.

Looking round he quickly realised that somehow half the town seemed to be rising up into the air – he wan't safe at all! And he had brown sauce all over him!

For the many people who weren't in the part of the town that was rising into the air, the first they knew about it was when day turned to night in the middle of the day.

Many had to put the living-room big light on. It was that bad!

Walking out to see where the sun had gone, they saw a huge chunk of their town rising up out of the ground. It was blocking out the sun!

"I bet Dennis has got something to do with this," many correctly guessed.

WE NEED TO START THINKING ABOUT MERCHANDISE

So things on Earth weren't going well.

Things in space weren't going well either. At least not for Lady BigBad.

The aliens were meant to be invading Earth in two orns (two orns is about half a day) and she *so* did not like getting behind schedule.

They'd teleported a human warrior up for the battle arena. (Lady BigBad and her teleportation technicians had scanned Earth for a warrior and had seen Minnie on the golf course, fighting imaginary aliens with the flag, and thought she was an Earth warrior practising her moves.)

Minnie's fight in the arena was supposed to show the BigBad Alliance's Elder Council (the proper big, scary bosses back home) how easily humans would be beaten, but it now seemed that invading Earth wouldn't be easy at all!

Lady BigBad should have known. The human called Minnie had shown unusual confidence since the first moment she'd arrived. (Lady BigBad didn't know that this was only through not understanding the danger she was in.) Now it was clear that humans were unbelievably good at fighting.

As you know this was another misunderstanding. Humans weren't that great at fighting. The fighters in the battle arena used to fight as a punishment. Many of the bigger, badder ones found they liked it. Due to being big and bad. The little squishy aliens weren't so keen.

Now they all assumed that Minnie had been sent to them to make their fights more entertaining. This was mostly because of the "Minnie effect". That odd thing that happens around Minnie where people (and now aliens) get carried away with Minnie's imagination. She's a very infectious and confusing girl to be around.

And the fights were much more entertaining. They weren't actually real anymore, but the crowd was loving it.

Backstage was also much nicer. The small  aliens, who had been sent there as punishment for often really small crimes like putting a drinks can in the bin for waste paper, were no longer afraid. The big bad aliens were now being friendly with them. There was a real team spirit vibe as they all worked out their moves and routines.

Their regular battles in the arena now felt more like dancing than fighting. And no one was getting hurt!

Backstage, a few hours after her first fight, Minnie was workshopping some new moves as Blerch the guard entered. She was showing a thing that looked like a cross between a hedgehog and a giraffe how to bring down a... (I have no idea how to describe it. I'm not that good a writer.)

"Lady BigBad wants to see you," snarled Blerch, as he saw her take down the creature that was easily twice her size. The other creatures looked at each other. What did the regional leader want with their new instructor, they wondered.

"Aw, great!" Minnie replied without hesitation. "I need a chat. We need to start thinking about merchandise!" And she strode confidently out of the cells, as though she wasn't even afraid of Lady BigBad.

Was it possible they were actually friends? This idea made everyone suddenly quite afraid of Minnie. Any friend of the terrifying Lady BigBad had to be frightening too! The smallest punishment for the smallest crime was being sent to the battle arena. And that was really bad. So no one was going to ask a question for fear of getting shouted at or much, much worse.

Now believing that Minnie was an incredibly important being, the guards Borf and Blerch gently and respectfully showed Minnie into Lady BigBad's chamber. Lady BigBad saw how afraid Borf and Blerch were of her and thought, wrongly, that she must have fought them and kicked their butts.

"Sup, girlfriend?" Minnie asked.

Borf and Blerch both respectfully backed out of the chamber and closed the door.

Minnie heard it lock. She saw a panel next to the door – you needed a four-digit code to unlock it. One of the code numbers was accidentally showing, though, which gave her a clue to the other three digits. Minnie figured out the passcode pretty quickly, but stayed put. She wanted a chat with the big boss.

Can you figure out the three numbers to unlock the door?

Answer: The middle number is the sum of the numbers above and below, or to each side. So the first number is 9 (2+7=9 or 4+5=9) You can figure out the middle number, but what is the bottom number?

"I've decided not to invade your planet," Lady BigBad told Minnie.

"Oh, right." This invading thing was new to Minnie. "Good, I guess."

"While it seems our best soldiers would be able to subdue a human in a simple one-to-one fight, there are seven billion humans on your planet and I only have a million soldiers."

Lady BigBad was tough, ruthless even, but not power mad like Mayor Wilbur and his son Walter. She was professional and businesslike in her evilness. Invading Earth was just going to cost too much.

"Er, okay," said Minnie, feeling the same way she usually felt at school if she'd not been listening before the teacher asked a question.

Minnie still hadn't realised she'd saved the world (and we're only just over halfway through the book!).

Lady BigBad had new plans for Minnie. She'd

arrived as a nobody but in the space of a few hours and with only one fight had become feared and respected by the underlings around her. She could be very useful to Lady BigBad. Perhaps, one day, as a general?

"So... am I being sent home?" Minnie asked. She thought it was probably nearly dinner time.

"No," Lady BigBad told Minnie. "You'll remain here forever. You're already very popular in the battle arena."

Lady BigBad was about to get to the good bit where she would offer Minnie a life of luxury, but—

"Forever?!" Minnie stormed forwards. "Forever will make me late for—" But before she could say "dinner", Minnie ran into... nothing.

The nothing was like a glass wall, but completely undetectable. There was an invisible force field across the entire room.

Lady BigBad wasn't stupid. She wanted something in between her and this human warrior.

Minnie was angry. "You can't keep me here!" she shouted, rubbing her forehead. "The last time I was late home for dinner, Mum hit the roof!"

One word in that sentence stood out for Lady BigBad... "Mum". In seconds, Lady BigBad's dreams of Minnie helping her rule this part of space with an iron fist evaporated.

"Are you a child?" she asked. Lady BigBad had assumed Minnie was a grown adult of her species. She'd never actually seen a human in real life, so didn't know what a child looked like.

"Of course I'm a kid!" Minnie shouted. "And if I'm not home for dinner, Mum will want to know why!"

Lady BigBad suddenly remembered something else Minnie had just said: "Mum hit the roof!" How big were female adult humans? Human buildings were mostly really high.

Lady BigBad now saw that this small human alien, who even the guards were afraid of, was related to much bigger human aliens. How scary must they be? Luckily the city ship was safe here in space. Adult humans couldn't get them up here.

Lady BigBad's assistant, Ploop, burst into the chamber through a side door (on Lady BigBad's side of the force field). Ploop was carrying a large (for the small alien) video screen.

"Your excellency! A large craft is headed this way from Earth, on an **attack** vector!" Ploop said in a panicked tone.

Lady BigBad grabbed the screen and studied it. It was hard to believe what she was seeing. "This is the town that she's from!" Lady BigBad said, gesturing towards Minnie.

Ploop and Lady BigBad looked at Minnie, who didn't seem in the slightest bit surprised.

Minnie shrugged and said, "Why wouldn't the town fly into space to get me back? I'm Minnie the Minx!"

THIS IS ALL PRETTY MUCH DENNIS'S FAULT

Earlier, back on Earth... No, hold on. That's not right. Beanotown wasn't actually on Earth anymore. Earlier, back in Beanotown, people had been worried. It's natural to be worried when the town you're in starts flying. Dennis's dad's emotions were similar to a lot of residents.

He rushed home with the milk and a squashed loaf, burst in, found his wife and blurted out, "The town's flying! Actually flying! Do we have parachutes?"

Dennis's mum looked at him. "What's that on your shirt?" she asked.

"Brown sauce," Dennis's dad told her. "Never mind about that. The important thing is the town is flying! Where are the parachutes? Are they in with the duvet covers?"

"How'd you get brown sauce all up your shirt

like that?" she asked, frowning.

"This..." her husband said, gesturing to all the sauce (and it was quite a lot) "... is not important! Not compared with the fact that the town is flying! If we don't have parachutes, get on YouTube and find out how to make parachutes out of duvet covers!"

"The Wi-Fi's off. Remember?" Dennis's mum answered. "And I'm not using up all my data on videos!"

"THE WI-FI!" Dad shouted. "Is Wi-Fi what keeps the town from flying away? It went off and now we're flying... They have to be connected!"

They were connected.

If the Wi-Fi had been working, Dad wouldn't have shown Dennis how to make a pop-bottle rocket.

If he hadn't done that, Dennis wouldn't have gone into the woods chasing after the bottle and he wouldn't have fallen down the hole and found the jets.

There's so much more that's Dennis's fault

too, though. If you remember, the Wi-Fi breaking was caused by a huge power surge that blew the system. Out in space, something detected that huge power surge. Something that hadn't noticed Earth before... the BigBad Alliance! Which led to Minnie getting teleported.

Luckily for Dennis, no one ever figures any of this out.

Over on the golf course, Mayor Wilbur wasn't worried. He was feeling impatient.

"The town's flying. A little earlier than I would have liked, but what really matters now is that we fly the town to the Caribbean. How do you steer this thing?"

Dennis was standing near enough to hear this and thought it was a cool idea. The Caribbean was where all those pirate movies came from.

"Then we can push all the poor people off, into the sea, and sell their homes to millionaires. Beanotown Island will be a paradise for the rich, and I'll be the Mayor of that paradise!"

"WHAT?" Dennis shouted.

He knew for a fact that his family was not rich. At least once a day he would break (or Gnasher would chew through) something, and whichever parent found out would say something like, "We can't afford a new one!"

Dennis suddenly had a mission. At all costs, he had to stop the Mayor!

Which, as the writer of this, I'm personally glad about. Finally we have Dennis on one side and the Mayor on the other. We've got a proper goodie-baddie story happening at last!

"Land this town now!" Dennis demanded,

over the sound of the increasing wind, that was quickly becoming a gale.

"Absolutely not!" answered the Mayor. "We're going to the Caribbean!"

"You idiots!" shouted a desperate scientist, clambering out of the hole he'd dug. "We can't shut the jets off or steer!"

Dennis turned back to the Mayor. "You can't stop this?" he asked him.

"He can't stop anything!" the scientist answered. "The town's headed into space! Once we leave Earth's gravity there'll be nothing to pull us back to Earth. This wind isn't wind! It's the air leaving the town! We all need to start making space suits now!"

To which everyone, goodies and baddies and those in between, agreed.

And with that, my hopes of a proper, simple goodie-baddie story evaporated.

2KG

If a scientist's spade carries 2 kg of earth and the scientist can dig 15 spades in one minute, after 10 minutes how many kilograms of earth will be in the hole?

Answer: There'll be 0 kg of earth in the hole. It's a hole!

THOSE PLASTIC TUBE THINGIES

An unrealistically short period of time later, Dennis and Gnasher burst into their house.

"MUM! DAD!" Dennis called, frantically looking for them. "What's that all over your shirt, Dad?" Dennis asked, once he found them in the kitchen.

"Brown sauce," Mum replied, tutting.

"It doesn't matter about the sauce!" Dad protested, doing nothing to stop Gnasher, who was greedily licking his shirt. "There are bigger things happening!"

"Dad's right," Dennis told them. "The town's headed into space! We need to make space suits, now."

"What?!" Mum and Dad shouted.

"Soon we'll all be in the vacuum of space!" Dennis warned his parents. Thinking aloud, he said:

"Vacuum? Vacuum! Where's the vacuum thingy? That's a good start! They've got tubes!"

What followed, in every household in the flying bit of Beanotown, was a frantic race against time to invent makeshift space suits out of household objects. Popular items for use were goldfish bowls, shower curtains, wellies, plastic containers, those plastic tube thingies that you wave around your head and they make **woooOOOOoooOOOOoo** sound, motorbike helmets, rubber gloves, garden hoses, beach inflatables, empty pop bottles, gaffer tape, elastic bands, and...

"Fishing waders!" Dad blurted out as he staggered back from the garage with arms full of useful junk. "I've got fishing waders in the shed. HA HA!" He then fake-laughed while pointing at Mum. "And you said they were a waste of money!"

Mum quickly fashioned a clear space suit out of a shower curtain for Dennis. Dennis strapped the TV remote to his wrist with elastic bands, to give his suit a futuristic vibe.

In a surprisingly short time, the family were suited up. It had taken lots of gaffer tape and the large selection of wellies Mum had been sorting

that morning, but they were ready.

Dennis and Gnasher had roomy suits that had a lot of extra space in them for spare air. Dad had extra plastic food boxes to store air in and Mum was using pop bottles. To Dennis's horror, she had just poured the pop into the sink.

And Dennis's sister
Bea was safely sealed up
in her pushchair's plastic
rain cover. Each member
of the family was airtight
in their own pocket of
oxygen.

Everyone was really quite
comfortable apart from Dad,
who had an ex-vacuum body
as a helmet. You could see his
chubby cheeks squashed up
against the plastic. He also
wasn't happy about the
quality of his air. One
of the Tupperware
containers he was using
for air storage had been
used for egg mayo and hadn't
been properly washed.

As the town left the Earth's atmosphere, no one questioned why the town kept its gravity. When you're running out of air, air tends to be the only thing you think about, but any other town in the world would have lost its gravity in space. Beanotown didn't because the park was in the middle, and in the middle of the park is the duck pond, and in the middle of that is Duck Island, and in the middle of Duck Island is the asteroid that, with its incredible gravity field, due to its own strange properties, has shrunk a prehistoric world, complete with dinosaurs, down to the size of a driveway. It was this separate and unique gravity well that was keeping everyone stuck to Beanotown, but like I say, when you're running out of air, all you think is **ARRRGH! AIR!**

Dennis said to his parents, "Is it alright if me and Gnasher go out and maybe try to get Beanotown back to Earth?"

"I wish you would," said Mum. "There's only

about an hour's air supply in these suits."

Which is impossible by the way. Sound doesn't travel in a vacuum, so they shouldn't have been able to hear each other. But Mum had forgotten you can't have conversations in the vacuum of space, and Dennis hadn't learnt that yet.

Dennis opened his mouth to tell Mum about the thing one of the scientists had said, that soon the town would leave Earth's gravity and then there'd be no hope of getting back. Dennis then closed his mouth again. Mum didn't need to know that as bad as things seemed, they were actually worse.

Dennis and Gnasher ran out of the house. Their mission was clear: they had one hour to get Beanotown back down to Earth. Somehow.

But that plan went totally out of the window when they stepped outside and looked up into the sky.

At this time of day, in summer, there should have been blue skies with, perhaps, a few fluffy

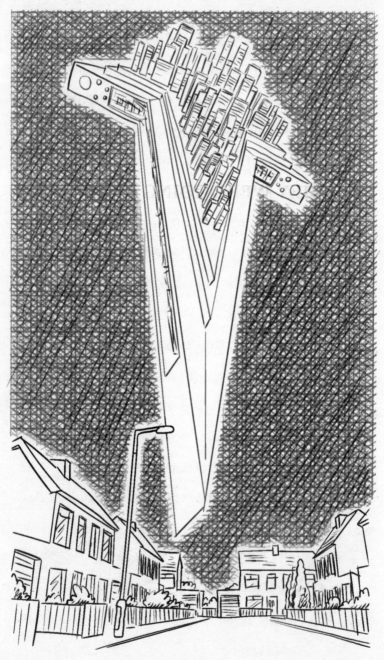

clouds. Instead, they saw a black sky, mostly filled with a giant star-shaped spaceship.

And the enormous spaceship above them was getting bigger and bigger as they flew directly towards it.

THEY WERE GOING TO CRASH!!!

CALL THE WAR OFF!
I'M BACK!

"Launch all attack fighters!" Lady BigBad shouted into the communication panel on her desk.

Minnie was shocked. The Alliance had started all this when they teleported her up here. Now they were getting all overreacty.

Lady BigBad turned to Minnie to say something evil and worrying and scary... but Minnie wasn't there!

Minnie had used the code she'd figured out earlier to unlock the door, and had quickly run out into the hall and grabbed Blerch the guard.

"YOU!" she shouted. "I need an attack fighter! Take me to the attack-ship hangar, and be quick about it. There'd better be one left for me!"

"Follow me, madam," Blerch replied, keen to impress Lady BigBad's friend. "The hangar is in this building, just two floors down."

And with that, they both rushed off to get Minnie an attack fighter.

Back in her chamber, Lady BigBad rushed towards the door after Minnie, but ran straight into the invisible force field and knocked herself out.

Ploop saw this and tootled over to her evil mistress.

"Er, Missus Bad?" Ploop asked nervously. "Are you okay?"

Lady BigBad started snoring.

Minnie strode into the hangar bay, then quickly stopped.

"What are those?" she said, pointing at a rack of flight suits.

"Flight suits," Blerch told her. "They're pretty good. They work in a vacuum."

"Nice!" exclaimed Minnie. "You got any in red and black?"

The guard smiled. "You'll need a helmet too," he said.

It was only when Minnie was climbing the ladder to get into her attack fighter that she realised she didn't know how to fly a spaceship.

She plonked down into the seat and was shocked, but also relieved, to see that the controller for the ship was almost the same as the controller for her Not-Tendo Itch Box 2!

Minnie pressed X and the ship's engines burst into life and it shot out of the hangar bay (which meant circle was probably fire).

Minnie pulled back hard on the controller. Unlike a Not-Tendo, this controller was connected to the floor by a stick. As Minnie pulled back, the sleek craft soared up and up.

Once she was quite far from the city ship, Minnie tipped the attack fighter and looked down.

The city ship was trying to reverse away from the fast-approaching section of Beanotown. It looked like all the BigBad's retro-jets (not trendy, old-fashioned jets but small jets for going backwards) were full on, but they were too small. The two huge objects were going to hit each other.

From her high vantage point, Minnie could see the other attack fighters headed for Beanotown. They were obviously hoping that if they zapped the town enough, Beanotown would call off their attack.

Minnie knew the only thing that would stop

the town attacking was her safe return. If she could land her fighter in the town hall square and show everyone she was back, she could stop an interstellar war. (Again.)

Imagine being that self-confident. Imagine thinking you're that awesome. Thinking that everyone loved you so much that if you left town, the entire town, including the buildings and the dirt beneath them, would come after you!

In reality, most of the town didn't even know Minnie, and Minnie's own parents – having taped themselves into their car as a quick oxygen pod – weren't expecting her home for tea for another half hour. Which reminded Minnie's mum...

"Dinner's in the oven! It'll get burnt!" she exclaimed.

"Relax!" said Minnie's dad. "Fire can't burn in space. It needs oxygen."

"Phew!" said Mum, relaxing a bit. "What are we going to have for dinner then?"

Dad looked in the glove box. "Wine gums!" he announced with triumph. His face fell into disappointment as he looked in the bag. "Oh, it's just the black ones left!"

The BigBad pilots had expected Beanotown to send out their own attack fighters, but they weren't. (It was almost as if the town didn't have its own fleet of attack fighters.) So instead of fighting their human enemy they opted for blowing random stuff up.

PEW! Boom! The left side of Bash Street School was obliterated.

PEW! Boom! WIDL's roof came flying off.

PEW! PEW! PEW!

Minnie fired at the lead fighter as she dived down into Beanotown. BigBad's lead ship was knocked off course and crashed into an estate agents.

Minnie raced down Beanotown Main Street, a lot like, er... you know, whatsisname. In that film where the young space-farmer kid flies down a narrow corridor on that big round space station that can blow up planets, so he can drop a bomb down the hole and blow it up? It was like that. But different enough to keep us all out of court.

In an incredible bit of unbelievable luck, Minnie landed her ship expertly in front of the town hall.

She opened the cockpit, stood up and shouted,

"It's alright! Call the war off! I'm back!"

Then she choked and gasped for air – because there was none – sat back down and shut the cockpit. The cockpit quickly filled up with air again and Minnie breathed in as much of it as she could.

"Note to self," she said. "Next time put your helmet on!"

Then, **BOOM!**, Beanotown crashed into the BigBad Alliance's city ship.

PEW PEW PEWING

Luckily it wasn't that big a bump. The city ship's retro-jets had managed to stop and reverse the city's movement so that it was now going in the same direction as Beanotown, just not quite fast enough to stop the bump.

Every building on both the city ship and in Beanotown shook, and Walter was thrown off his feet.

Yeah, that's right – Walter.

Dennis's lifelong enemy.

Walter had dealt with Beanotown going into space quite easily. Last summer they'd gone on holiday to the Caribbean and his dad – Wilbur, the Mayor – had gone scuba diving. But Walter's dad never rents anything. Especially scuba gear. He wasn't about to let anything that may have been near someone else's chops near his own lips. So he'd bought a new set. Which meant there were things like oxygen tanks and masks and rubber suits in Walter's garage.

A few hours ago, Wilbur had rung to warn him that the town would soon be in space. As the town hall was nearby, Wilbur had decided to lock himself in the enormous airtight walk-in safe.

"You have an enormous airtight walk-in safe?!" Walter had asked upon hearing this.

"Er... No?" Wilbur had answered, hanging up.

Then later, as you know, the BigBad Alliance's city ship crashed into Beanotown.

When two town-sized things bump into each other, they're going to touch somewhere. And that somewhere was Walter's front garden.

Walter, who was by now wearing scuba gear, looked up as attack fighters shot over head, towards Beanotown, their laser blasters **pew pew pewing**. Walter could see explosions in the background and imagine the horrible destruction.

Then he realised that one of these fighters could also take him back to Earth. That settled it. He had to get one.

And with that, he simply hopped onto the BigBad Alliance's city ship.

There was a momentary odd sensation as the gravity changed angle and he almost fell, but quickly he was running up – or was it along? – the pointiest point of the ship, towards the buildings on it.

As Walter approached the first building, he

passed through a strange dizzy patch where, for a moment, it was hard to see properly. Then he was through. Soon after, he noticed aliens in the city around him without breathing equipment.

Do aliens need to breathe? he thought. And suddenly he realised what the dizzy bit was: an invisible force field that kept the air in. Cautiously, Walter took the scuba mouthpiece out and tried a breath. He was relieved to find there was indeed air to breathe on the city ship.

More attack fighters zipped over his head on the way to Beanotown. Walter jogged off to where they were coming from.

HAVING TROUBLE, MATE?

Dennis and Gnasher ran down Main Street towards the colossal elongated star-shaped city that was poking Beanotown. They had no idea how they were meant to be sorting this problem out.

How do you fight a city?

How long does the air last in homemade space suits?

Ahead, they were surprised to see one of the attack fighters sticking half out of an estate agents! The cockpit was open, and the not-too-bright alien pilot had the engine cover off and was looking at the engine quizzically.

"Having trouble, mate?" Dennis asked helpfully.

"Yeah," the alien admitted. "I got blasted, knocked off course and crashed. I can't see any damage, but the thing won't start!"

If Dennis had thought more, he would have wondered how he and the alien could understand each other. (The attack fighter had its own mini translator installed.) But Dennis wasn't big on thinking more.

"Oh shame," said Dennis, looking over the alien's shoulder.

Attack-fighter engines looked tricky, but Dennis thought he saw the problem straight away. There was a disc in the middle of the engine that had "MAX LOAD 19 AMPS" marked on it. Above that was an arrow pointing to nothing in particular, which seemed odd to Dennis.

Leading to the disc were four wires, each with four lights on them. It seemed to Dennis that the arrow should probably point to one of the wires. That might be where the power came in.

"The crash probably just knocked the arrow thing off wherever it's meant to point," Dennis suggested.

"Ah, right," the alien said. "I think I remember this from training. The wrong setting will overload the engine and it'll trip out."

Dennis didn't know what "trip out" meant.

"Do you want me to get in?" Dennis suggested. "You try the different settings, and I'll try to get it started."

"Thanks, kid!" the alien said.

Dennis and Gnasher hopped into the cockpit.

"Try it now," the alien said to Dennis, after twisting the arrow.

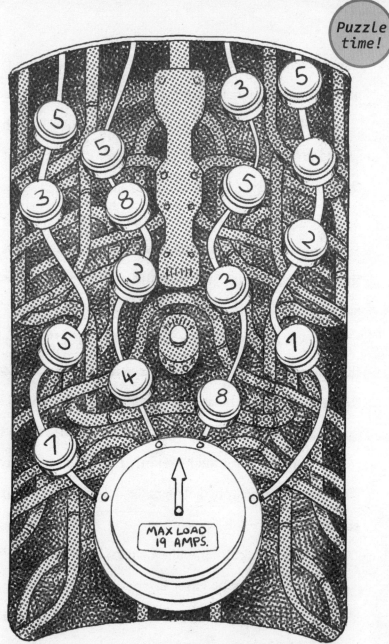

Too much power will blow the ship's fuse. Which setting will not add up to over 19 amps?

174

Dennis pressed X.

Nothing happened. It must have been overloaded.

"Naw, it's not that one," Dennis told the alien helpfully.

The alien tried another position, and suddenly the ship burst into life. It juddered forwards, breaking a bit more of the estate agents. The alien hopped back out of the way and laughed.

"We did it!" he shouted. "Thanks, kid!"

Dennis and Gnasher evil-grinned at each other, and they shot off down Main Street at 162 miles per hour.

The alien watched his attack fighter quickly disappear and groaned. It's not every day you help someone pinch your own ship.

Dennis and Gnasher laughed as they sped away. "What an intergalactic idiot!" Dennis said to his faithful hound.

Dennis and Gnasher were headed in the

wrong direction. Dennis pulled back hard on the controller and the ship rose quickly out of the town, zipping over the town hall just before doing so.

There was a lot to see and do. So it's unsurprising that Dennis failed to spot that he'd actually just flown over Minnie.

He and Gnasher completed a giant loop the loop and smoothly swooped down into the alien cityscape. Dennis hadn't really realised that he could instantly fly a spaceship and that the controller was nearly the same as his Not-Tendo at home. He just automatically accepted it. Years of gaming had convinced him he was brilliant at flying attack fighters. It felt completely natural.

Rocketing down the city ship's main street he saw a rather surprising thing. Huge video posters of Minnie! Close-ups of her striking poses, with alien words above and below her.

Dennis pressed the box button and the fighter screeched to a halt in front of one particularly large

poster. Minnie was clearly famous among aliens. What had she been doing?

Whatever it was, Dennis knew one thing for sure. Minnie was on board the alien ship. (He was wrong about that.)

The plan was now to save Minnie (which he didn't need to do) and send the aliens back to space. And then return Beanotown old town to Earth.

"How do I do that?" Dennis asked Gnasher.

Do what? Gnasher thought. Everything before "How do I do that?" had been inside Dennis's own head.

Without any sort of plan, Dennis aimed for the biggest building on the city ship. He flew over Walter as he did so – who was headed for the same place.

In his huge walk-in safe in the town hall, Mayor Wilbur was the safest of all the inhabitants of Beanotown. There was quite a lot of air inside the vault.

I'll be fine in here for days! he thought smugly.

Then he realised he needed a wee.

H-H-H-H-H-HUMAN!

So far, Dennis had been lucky.

If you'd seen his moves, you would have assumed that he was a brilliant pilot. If you did that, you'd be assuming wrong. Dennis was a terrible pilot who just hadn't crashed yet.

Then Dennis and Gnasher crashed.

The idea had been to swoop his fighter into the hangar bay halfway up the building. What happened was he stuffed it in through a window. If you then described what he did as "flying down a corridor, deep into the building", you'd be making it sound better than it was. It was more like "scraping and gouging down a corridor, deep into the building, until it boshed through the double doors at the end".

I still don't think I'm getting across the damage Dennis did to the walls, floor and ceiling of the corridor. The ship cut deep grooves into the floor, ripped enormous holes in the walls and brought down half the ceiling, bringing ducting, wiring and pipes down with it.

Gnasher gave Dennis a sideways look.

That'll be fine. A lick of paint will sort that right out, no trouble, he thought, as chunks of wall and ceiling fell down around them.

Lady BigBad – who, as you remember, had knocked herself out earlier – woke up.

While Lady BigBad got to her feet, Ploop pointed a trembling finger at Dennis and Gnasher.

"H-h-h-h-h-human!" Ploop said. **"A-a-and... THING!"** Ploop didn't have a name for whatever Gnasher was.

"I can see that," Lady BigBad said, dusting herself off. A possible enemy may have crashed in through the door, but that was no reason to panic.

A human boy, similar in size to Minnie, fell out of the small craft's cockpit, dropping and smashing his goldfish-bowl helmet as he did so. He had a spiky mop of black hair on his head and was closely followed by a completely spiky hairy creature, which hopped out rather gracefully.

"Urrgh!" groaned Dennis, looking at his shattered helmet. "I'm gonna need that later."

Lady BigBad had a general air of "I'm in charge" about her.

"Are you in charge?" Dennis asked.

"Of course I am!" Lady BigBad answered,

wondering if all humans wore red-and-black striped jumpers. And that hair – was that used for attack or defence?

Dennis stormed forwards. "Right! Well you need to..."

He ran into the invisible force field. (Remember that?)

He didn't knock himself out, though. Dennis's skull is much thicker than Lady BigBad's.

Dennis rubbed his forehead.

Gnasher smirked and said, "You ran into an invisible force field, didn't you?"

"ARRRGH!" Dennis shouted to his dog. **"YOU CAN TALK!"**

Gnasher was surprised at this. He didn't think he was speaking human. He thought he was gnashing and barking as normal.

"Am I human talking?" Gnasher asked. "You can understand me, can you? Red lorry, yellow lorry... The rain in Spain, falls mainly on the plain... You're getting all that, are you?"

"Buddy!" Dennis said. "You're talking normal... Well, you sound a bit posh actually!"

"Of course I'm a bit posh!" said Gnasher, "I'm an Abyssinian Wire-haired Tripe Hound, you know!"

The building's universal translator was translating Gnasher's gnashes. Dennis's ship had a translator too, as did all attack fighters, but Gnasher had only been thinking during their flight so they hadn't realised.

"You must have something you want to say to me," Dennis said. "After all these years!"

"I do," said Gnasher. "Can I have another one of those fishy biscuits?"

Dennis gave Gnasher two.

Before the conversation could go anywhere meaningful, something outside the window caught Lady BigBad's attention. Dennis followed her line of sight. Across the city, above the buildings, an object was growing bigger. Something was coming straight for them!

"That's another attack fighter!" Gnasher said, his face full of fish biscuit. "If it doesn't change course, it's going to crash into the window!"

"Come on, Gnasher," Dennis said to his faithful

hound, and he jumped back into his ship. As Dennis tried to get it going, Gnasher hopped in behind him.

The attack fighter was getting bigger and bigger, and Lady BigBad wasn't moving! (She knew there was no glass in the window. It was another unbreakable force field.)

Chugga-chugga-chugga! went Dennis's engine.

"Arrrgh!" Dennis shouted in frustration.

"This thing stops working every time it crashes!"

"Don't crash then!" said Gnasher unhelpfully.

Dennis couldn't help but worry about Mum, Dad and Bea back home. How long had it been since he'd left them at home? How much longer would the air in their homemade space suits last? It wouldn't be ages. And how close was the town to leaving Earth's gravity? Had it already happened? Was getting back already impossible? Dennis shook his head. It was something he didn't know, so he shouldn't worry about it. There were enough things to think about.

Chugga-chugga-chugga!

The ship headed for them turned over, dropped slightly and shot up past the window, centimetres away from the glass. For a brief moment you could see into the craft's cockpit. It was Minnie, smiling and waving!

VA-VA-VROOOOM! At last, Dennis's attack fighter burst into life. He slammed it into reverse and – well, do you remember how much damage he caused getting in there? The gouges, scrapes and holes? It was so much worse coming out.

"That's nothing to worry about," said Gnasher. "They were probably going to redecorate soon anyway."

While Dennis was reversing, Lady BigBad was in her own personal lift. She was going down to the fighter hangar.

The dangerous warrior, Minnie, now somehow had a fighter, and so did the human boy. It was time to get into her own personal extra-special fighter and sort this out herself!

PING!

The lift arrived at the hangar bay. The doors slid open and revealed Lady BigBad's personal attack fighter.

Which shot off, out of the hangar, on its own.

Followed by its fighter drones...

Which needs quite a bit of explaining...

Lady BigBad's fighter has 10 fighter drones that go with it. They follow the fighter and all have laser blasters which can be aimed by the main fighter.

The drones have a few settings. You can set them to target several different objects at once, as a group, or they can be set to defence mode, where some will target anyone firing at you while others shield you. The coolest setting though is the "fire at anything I fire at" mode. Lady BigBad's ship also has 90 spare drones, kept in a rack, so they're quite disposable.

Got it? Oh, I thought it would take more explaining than that.

As Dennis scraped and gouged his way back out of the building, he thought of what to do next. Minnie didn't need saving anymore (if she ever had). The alien boss lady had run off.

"We need a new plan!" Dennis announced

loudly over the sound of the ship's jets revving in reverse. "This city ship thingy has got to be steered from somewhere. Let's find out where and, I dunno, like do something?"

"Great plan," said Gnasher. "Lots of detail. No way it can go wrong. You've worked out all the angles."

"Urrrgh! Gnasher! You've only been speaking

for two minutes and you're already being sarcastic!" said Dennis.

"Call me Captain Star Paws, seeing as we seem to be doing this space adventure thing," said Gnasher.

Finally Dennis and Gnasher's fighter made it out of the building. The moment it did, the engines stopped working again and the fighter tumbled down the side of the hangar building.

"WHAT DID I SAY ABOUT NOT CRASHING?!" shouted Gnasher. (Well, actually it was more like, "What did I say about not craaaaaaaashinggggggg?!")

THIS ISN'T GOING WELL

Dennis had that sick feeling in his stomach that he normally quite liked on rollercoasters but which wasn't so much fun when you're in an attack fighter falling down the side of a building.

"Just hit all the buttons!" Gnasher suggested.

"DO YOU WANNA DRIVE, CAPTAIN?!" Dennis shouted over his shoulder as he hit and pressed and poked every button he could see, as the ship caught the side of the building again and rolled over. Suddenly the engines burst into life again, upside down, and the fighter flew into the hangar and crashed again.

"You're crashing more than you're flying!" Gnasher pointed out in his posh pedigree accent.

"I don't have time for you to have a go at me!" Dennis said. "The town can't last much longer without air."

Dennis looked to his side. Through the window,

he saw the alien boss lady approaching.

"This isn't going well," Gnasher said. Dennis had kind of figured that out himself.

Lady BigBad walked over to the ship Dennis and Gnasher were in and turned it over, so it was the right way up. She just grabbed a bit of the fighter with her hand and turned it over. As if it wasn't incredibly heavy.

Once the ship was the right way up, she opened the cockpit. I say "opened" – she wrenched it open.

"You're pretty strong," Dennis commented, pointing out the obvious.

"Yeah. Do you work out?" Gnasher asked.

"There wasn't time for a proper introduction earlier," Lady BigBad said. "I'm Lady BigBad. This is my city."

"Nice to meet you," said Gnasher. **"I'm Captain Star Paws."**

Dennis looked at Gnasher, "Are you really

sticking with that?" he asked.

"Shut it, kid – people will write books about my adventures."

"Who's got my ship?" demanded Lady BigBad.

"I dunno," said Dennis, shrugging.

"There's a lot he doesn't know," said Captain Star... No. I'm not doing that... said Gnasher.

"This talking thing you're doing is starting to bug me!" Dennis said to his fuzzy friend.

Lady BigBad reached into the cockpit and pressed a few buttons on the dashboard. The dash made a phone-ringing sound.

It rang and rang while Dennis, Gnasher and Lady BigBad hung around in awkward silence.

Eventually, whoever Lady BigBad was calling answered.

"Hello?" said Walter.

"Urrgh!" Dennis groaned.

"Dennis?" Walter asked. "Is that you?! How are you calling me?"

"He's not!" Lady BigBad interrupted. "I am! You're in my ship! I'd like it back."

"Oh, sorry, but I'm not going to do that," Walter replied. "This ship's mine now. I'm going to use it to go back to Earth!" Then Walter's tone changed, as if he was talking to himself. "I need to rescue Father first... or do I? I should. I'd feel bad if I didn't... or would I? No. I should almost certainly save Father... and **MOTHER!** I forgot Mother! Woah. Is this thing still on?"

The phone went dead.

"Is he your leader?" Lady BigBad asked.

"WHAT?! NO!" Dennis protested. "Walter's my, er... Well, he sees me as his enemy, but to me he's just annoying."

"Is he dangerous?" Lady BigBad asked.

"Usually, no," Gnasher answered. "But if he's got your fighter, then yes. He's extremely dangerous!"

The best thing to fight a human would be another human, Lady BigBad thought.

"What's it gonna take for you to call off this invasion?" Dennis asked, interrupting her train of thought.

Lady BigBad, if you remember, had already called the invasion off.

"I'll call it off if you turn your city ship around and get me back my executive fighter," she replied.

My city ship? Dennis thought to himself,

What's she...

Then, out loud, he said: "Oh! You think Beanotown's a city ship! No, that's up here in space by accident. We don't know how to steer it."

Lady BigBad thought for a moment. This was good news. Humans may be dangerous warriors but it seemed none of them, apart from this Walter kid, were a danger to the Alliance right now. It would be best to help Dennis, Minnie and Gnasher make the whole human issue go away.

"My drone fighters could help. Ten of them are with my personal attack fighter, but there are actually another 90 kept as back-up. If they attach round the edge of your town, they could be used to steer it back to Earth."

"Well let's do that then!" Dennis agreed.

"We can't yet," Lady BigBad said. "They're all controlled from my ship.

"BUT WALTER HAS THAT!" Gnasher shouted.

"You catch on quick," Lady BigBad retorted. "If you promise to stay there, I'll help you and your town get back to Earth."

Dennis nodded and Gnasher bowed his head in agreement.

"You'll need the help of the galaxy's greatest warrior," said Lady BigBad.

"Er, yeah, okay," said Dennis. "Who's that?"

"I believe you know her as Minnie," she answered.

Gnasher was lost for words.

EPIC BATTLE TIME?
EPIC BATTLE TIME!

Where was Minnie?

There had been a brief moment, when Minnie realised Beanotown had no air, that she'd thought it should be sent back to Earth. So she'd set off to find a way to do that, but forgotten that was what she was meant to be doing 11 seconds later.

Instead, Minnie was flying aimlessly around the alien city.

She swooped between two dangerously close buildings. I can't express enough that you shouldn't do this at home. If you ever find an alien attack fighter, don't get in it. Don't fly it and especially don't fly it between close-together buildings for fun.

The phone rang in her fighter.

That sounds like a phone, Minnie thought.

It kept ringing. And rang some more.

The problem was, it wasn't obvious where it

was ringing from. There were the few buttons on the controller she'd pressed and pushed hundreds of times in the short time she'd been flying around. It was obvious it was none of them.

Then there were the hundreds of buttons on the dash in front of her. Any one of those could be the "accept call" button.

Minnie slapped the dashboard with the palm of her hand, trying to press as many buttons as possible at once. Horns sounded, windscreen wipers came on for a moment, and Dennis said, "Finally!"

"Hi Dennis!" Minnie said. "This is a thing isn't it?!"

"Yup!" Dennis agreed. "We need to save the town. Everybody in Beanotown's probably only got a few more minutes left." (He was right.)

"Right!" Minnie agreed. "Er... how?"

Dennis told her how the drones controlled by Lady BigBad's ship could steer Beanotown back to Earth.

"Nice! So let's do that then," said Minnie.

Dennis explained that Walter had the ship.

"Urrrrrrrrrrrrrrrrrrrrrrrrrrrrr..."
Minnie said, and didn't stop, "... rrrrrrrrrrrrrrrrrrr—"

"Alright! Give it a rest!" Dennis interrupted.

"... rrrrrgh!" Minnie finished. Then she added:
"Are we gonna bother asking him?"

"I suppose we should," said Dennis.

In Lady BigBad's ship, the phone rang.

"Hello?" answered Walter.

"Walter!" Dennis said. "Beanotown's running
out of air! We need that ship you're in. It controls
drones that could take the town back to Earth."

"Yeah, but this is mine now," Walter replied.

"The town needs it!" Minnie interrupted.
"Stop being such a loser!"

"I'm sure the town can figure it out
themselves," Walter said. "I need this ship to get
back to Earth and take over..."

He was going to say "Beanotown", but had

just realised it wasn't on Earth anymore.

"... take over..."

Then Walter said the name of the town you're living in now!

Dennis hung up. "Well, we tried!" he said.

"Epic battle time?" Minnie asked.

"Epic battle time!" Gnasher agreed.

"Wait!" said Minnie, hearing his voice over the communicator. "Who's that?"

"Captain Star Paws!" Gnasher answered.

Minnie imagined what Captain Star Paws looked like. She got it very wrong.

COME ON SIMON!
WHO'S SIMON?

Back at Dennis's house, Dad was starting to panic.

The air in his suit may have been eggy, but he still wanted more. It felt a lot like it was running out. (Because it was.)

"I'm running out of air!" he shouted, panicking and breathing in and out a lot.

"Calm down!" Mum said. "You're using up your air."

"We need to find more!" Dad said. "What's got air in it?"

Mum had already thought of the car as quite a big air store, but was saving it for later.

"Let's all share our air," she said calmly.

"How?" Dad asked, "Without letting any air out?"

Mum showed Dad how. Her suit and Bea's pod were now joined by a section of garden hose. It was quite easy. You simply taped a length of garden hose between two suits on weak points – like a bit where it's only tape – then once the hose was connected you pushed it through the tape.

A few moments later, Dad's suit was connected to Mum and Bea's.

"Urrgh!" said Mum, as she breathed in Dad's eggy air. "Have you let one off?"

"No!" Dad protested. "One of the containers had egg mayo in, and it hadn't been washed out properly!"

Mum and Bea looked at Dad suspiciously.

"Honest!"

This was Dennis's fault. They'd made the mistake of asking him to do the washing up.

A couple of streets away, Minnie's parents were doing a little better.

They'd taped themselves into their car on the driveway. Wisely, Minnie's dad had brought a house plant with them. He knew that plants breathe in what we breathe out, and breathe out what we breathe in. It was perched on his knees.

"Come on, Simon!" Minnie's dad urged the *Monstera deliciosa* (also known as a Swiss cheese plant). "Breathe!"

"Who's Simon?" Minnie's mum asked from the front seat.

"This is Simon," Minnie's dad said from the

back, caressing Simon's leaves. "He's giving us oxygen!"

Mum realised he was right, and turned round. "Come on, Simon! You can do it!" she urged.

This is a lot of pressure, thought Simon the cheese plant. I preferred it when I was just left in the corner of the living room!

"I do hope Minnie's alright," Mum said to Dad, looking out of the window.

Just then, Minnie shot down the street, centimetres from the tarmac, in her attack fighter. She swooped up and away again near the end of the street, disappearing from view and waving as she did so.

"I think she'll be alright," Minnie's dad replied.

NINETY-NINE DRONES

A couple of minutes earlier, **SHOOOF!** – an attack fighter had shot out of the hangar on the city ship.

Only one.

Chugga-chugga-chugga! went Dennis and Gnasher's ship, back in the hangar. Dennis opened the cockpit and turned to Lady BigBad.

"You haven't got a spare fighter I can borrow, have you?" he asked, with a sheepish grin on his face.

Lady BigBad rolled her eyes. "Do you want a flight suit too? That thing you're wearing looks a bit homemade, and you broke your helmet."

"Have you got anything in red and black?" Dennis asked.

Ahead of them, Minnie was chasing after Walter.

It looked like he was headed for the town hall in Beanotown.

"I'm gonna fly past my house, on the way!" she thought.

So that's how that thing happened where she did that.

Walter had reached the town hall and was hovering over it. He knew his father was safe in a safe inside, but how could he get him out without exposing him to the vacuum of space?

Looking out of his window, he had an idea. Could he use his special fighter drones to somehow lift the safe out of the town hall and—

PEW! PEW! PEW!

Laser blasts hit his ship. It was Minnie!

Father would have to wait. Before Walter could figure out how to fire back, the 10 drones surrounding his ship burst into action and fired back. (They were set on automatic defence mode, which fired at any nearby aircraft.)

Walter grinned.

He liked this ship.

Laser blasts pewed off Minnie's hull.

Yikes! she thought and pushed the controller forwards, dropping her ship behind some buildings for cover. I'll have to stay low and use the streets to get close.

The phone rang. It was Dennis.

"You'd better not be firing at Walter!" he shouted.

"Of course I am!" Minnie answered. "What part of 'epic battle' do you not understand?"

"If we wreck that ship it won't be able to

control the back-up drones to take Beanotown back to Earth!" Gnasher warned her.

"Oh, right!" said Minnie sarcastically. "So we're supposed to defeat Walter in an epic space battle without zapping him? Great! I'll get right on that! Is it okay if I hit his spaceship with a pillow?"

SHOOF!

Minnie looked up and saw an attack fighter zip overhead. Dennis and Gnasher had caught her up.

PEW! PEW! PEW!

Walter was firing at Dennis and Gnasher.

Dennis spun his ship, barrel rolling in an effort to avoid the laser bolts.

PEW! PEW! PEW!

Minnie fired back, catching a drone and destroying it.

"I said don't fire!" Dennis shouted over the comms link.

"I'm not firing!" Minnie shouted. "I'm firing back. There's a difference!"

"Well, don't!" added Gnasher. "We need those drones, and we're running out of time!"

Back at the hangar, one of the replacement drones woke up and zipped out of the hangar on its way to join the executive fighter. It was replacing the drone just destroyed by Minnie.

Lady BigBad saw this and called Dennis and Gnasher. "You're down to 99 drones," she informed them. "You need as many as possible to move your town."

"I know, I know!" Dennis answered. "Gimme a break – this job's kinda impossible. And where are your other fighters, to help us?"

"No," said Lady BigBad unhelpfully.

"I thought we were on the same side now!" said Dennis.

"You thought wrong," Lady BigBad replied. "This fight's between yourselves. Now I know your town's here by accident and we're not at war, I'll not risk any of my own pilots. But good luck, human."

"Gee, thanks!" Dennis shouted before hanging up.

Unaware that Minnie and Dennis were no longer going to fire on him, Walter zipped off towards the library. He was hoping he'd be harder to hit, as a moving target.

Minnie and Dennis gave chase.

In the executive fighter, Walter was trying to get to grips with the drone controls. Unable to figure out any of the buttons, he tried something else.

"Computer?" he asked.

"Yes?" the onboard computer answered.

Walter grinned a wicked grin. "Tell me about these drone thingies. How do they work, and what exactly can I do with them?"

THAT'S NOT A PLAN

On his rear-view screen, Walter saw Dennis and Minnie chasing after him.

"Computer, set drones to attack mode," he commanded. He'd just learned about attack mode, and it sounded like it might be his favourite.

The drones switched mode from defensive

(just firing back) to attack (going after any threat). All around his ship, the jet-powered drones flipped round, pointing backwards.

PEW! PEW! PEW!

They fired at Dennis, Gnasher and Minnie.

"I've got a plan!" Dennis told Minnie. "I'll try to get in front of Walter." (That's not a plan – it's just doing one thing without knowing what it'll lead to.)

"Awesome! Go for it!" Minnie said, whose idea of what a plan was was even sketchier than Dennis's.

Minnie whizzed off, out of sight.

Dennis dropped down to street level, so he was hidden by the buildings. Walter raced on towards the library. In an effort to distract him, Dennis called Walter on the phone.

"Walter, stop being such an idiot!" he said. "You need to save your parents, don't you? Taking Beanotown back to Earth is the only way!"

Annoyingly, Walter knew this was true, but

didn't want to admit it. And he really, really, really didn't want to give up the amazing spaceship he was in. Especially now he'd just discovered attack mode. There was also no way he was ever going to admit Dennis was right!

"Of course I'm going to save my parents," Walter shouted back. "I'm going to use these drone things to save them. They'll be fine!"

While this conversation was going on, Minnie was chasing after Walter. Dennis had cut left and flown down Bash Street, in the hopes of cutting Walter off before they got as far as the comic shop. Dennis felt sure if he could get in front of Walter, er, you know... something might happen?

Something did happen.

Dennis (and Gnasher) crashed into Walter.

Dennis had assumed that when Walter saw their fighter coming straight for him, he'd brake. But Walter didn't, because he was looking behind him at Minnie.

PEW! PEW! PEW!

The drones were the first to spot Dennis and Gnasher, and fired at them. Then quickly, realising they were on a collision course, they turned and tried to get in the way.

One managed to do just that and was smashed to bits on the front of Dennis's ship.

But Dennis's fighter hardly slowed at all and – **CRASH!** – the two ships met and glanced off each other.

Walter spun out of control and crashed near the secondhand-games shop. Dennis and Gnasher, a couple of streets away, came down near the swimming pool.

Back at the hangar on the city ship, another one of the racked drones woke up and zipped out of the hangar, to replace the one that had just crashed into Dennis's ship.

Lady BigBad called Dennis again.

"Ninety-eight left," she informed him. "And

very little time left for the humans on your city ship. What are you doing out there?"

"I don't want to talk about it!" Dennis told her.

Walter pushed the start button on his controller, and the engine instantly restarted. He pulled back on the stick, and the craft shot back up—

He crashed straight into Minnie, who was zipping overhead, looking for them.

SMASH!

Another drone was destroyed, and another back-up drone unracked itself back at the hangar.

"Ninety-seven," Lady BigBad said to herself, rightly thinking Dennis probably didn't want to hear about it.

CHUGGA-CHUGGA-CHUGGA! went Dennis and Gnasher's ship.

"Urrrgh!" Dennis groaned to himself. "Why are attack fighters so delicate?"

Then he saw something. Something helpful.

That'll be helpful, he thought.

ATTACK MINNIE!

Meanwhile, the tables had turned between Minnie and Walter.

Walter was now chasing after Minnie.

"ALL ATTACK DRONES, ATTACK MINNIE!" he cruelly shouted at the ship's computer.

"Define 'Minnie'," the computer asked, in a voice way too calm for the current situation.

"THE HUMAN IN FRONT!" Walter shouted.

But you need to be careful when issuing orders to a computer. Computers don't assume what you mean, they just do what you say. And "all" drones kinda means all drones.

At the hangar, every single spare drone unracked itself and zipped out towards Walter in the executive fighter.

Lady BigBad raised an eyebrow. Thinking

that these drones were on their way to help guide Beanotown back, she said to herself, "Ah, they must have sorted it out."

But the situation was the opposite of sorted out.

PEW! **PEW!** **PEW!** went the 10 drones around Walter's ship.

Minnie skilfully avoided most of the blasts.

Then **PEW! PEW! PEW! PEW! PEW! PEW! PEW! PEW! PEW! PEW! PEW! PEW! PEW! PEW!** went a bunch of other drones.

Avoiding the laser blasts from 10 drones is tricky, but with luck it can be done. Avoiding the laser blasts from 98 drones is impossible.

Minnie pulled the stick right back. She was going straight up!

More than a hundred pews hit the underneath of her ship.

She felt the impacts through her feet. She

pulled back more, so that she was now upside down, flying back towards Walter.

Still upside down, Minnie's ship zipped over Walter's with only a few feet to spare.

The drones blasted apart her engines. Bits of Minnie's ship clattered down onto Walter's.

Walter looked behind him on the rear-view screen and saw Minnie's ship spiral into what was left of the school, crash and explode.

For a moment, Walter was shocked. Things had got too far out of control. Minnie may have been an enemy, but...

KNOCK! KNOCK! KNOCK!

Walter looked up through the glass. It was Minnie. She was on his ship!

She must have bailed out of her doomed fighter as she flew over him.

PEW! PEW! PEW! PEW! PEW!

The drones were firing at Walter! The ship Walter was in!

Minnie dodged the blasts and scrambled to the back of the executive fighter. Grabbing a pipe, she hung off the side, using one of the wings for cover.

PEW! PEW! PEW!

The drones kept firing at Walter. He screamed. Why were they attacking him?!

They weren't. As I said before, you need to be careful with your words when you give instructions to a computer. Earlier, Walter had told the drones to attack Minnie, not her ship. Now Minnie was on his ship, and it had become the target!

Walter completely failed to figure any of this out. As the drones tried to destroy the very thing that controlled them, and in doing so were destroying any hope of saving Beanotown, Walter just screamed.

So things are bad, right? They can't get worse, yeah?

Wrong.

THINGS GET WORSE.

Dennis flew low through the streets of Beanotown, towards the battle in the distance. There were a lot of shots being fired, but Dennis couldn't make out what exactly was happening.

As he moved forwards, he kept having to adjust the ship's course downwards. Time and again he had to push forwards on the stick to lower his fighter. It kept trying to go up, for some reason.

Walter's ship, ahead, was also rising. Dennis couldn't see Minnie's ship anywhere.

Once he was closer, Dennis could see that the "battle" was now just Walter's own drones firing at the executive fighter.

"What's that idiot done?!" Dennis exclaimed.

Tucked in the space behind Dennis's seat, Gnasher licked his teeth to check that he hadn't damaged them by gnashing through metal! (You'll find out what he was gnashing soon.)

The phone rang. It was Lady BigBad.

"Well done," she said. "Once you land, I'll teleport down to get my ship back, and we can all never see each other again."

"What do you mean, 'Well done'?" Dennis asked. "I'm still working on it!"

"Then why is your town returning to Earth?" Lady BigBad asked.

Something dawned on Dennis then. His and Walter's ships weren't going up – the entire town was going down.

Was this a good thing? Of course it was! It meant that the jets had stopped before the town had escaped Earth's gravity. Finally some good news!

"It's just going back on its own," Dennis said.

"Oh... right..." Lady BigBad said. "Well, you're welcome to stay on our city ship. You, Captain Star Paws and Minnie can stay at the battle arena. She's really quite popular."

Dennis didn't understand this, but he didn't

like the sound of it.

"Why would we want to live on your city ship?" Gnasher asked.

"If your town ship is going back to Earth without the drones, the jets must be running out of fuel. Your town is about to crash into Earth like a huge asteroid," Lady BigBad explained.

"Urrrrgh!" said Dennis. "That's great, that is!"

"Something that big hitting your planet will probably send it into a 10-year long winter. It'll throw so much dirt into your atmosphere you'll not see your sun for years."

Somewhere in the huge chunk of Earth that had come up into space with the town, there was a lake of jet fuel. Or at least there had been. And now the jets had used it all up!

"STOP TALKING!" Dennis shouted. **"ARRRGH!"** Dennis was angry. Life was stupid. Going off into space was bad. It was what they were trying to stop. Now the opposite of the bad thing was happening and somehow that was worse?!?!

Things had gone from very serious to double very serious!

WHAT'S GOING ON NOW?!

Beanotown had been close to escaping Earth's gravity when the fuel began to run out. So the gravity that was now pulling it back down was, for the moment, quite weak. There was still time to do something – though Dennis and Gnasher didn't have a clue what that might be.

Dennis had to think fast. Right now, Beanotown was moving slowly back to Earth, but with every metre, the power of Earth's pull increased, and so did its speed towards Earth.

Dennis decided to stick with his recent, and typically vague, plan: "Do something with the magnet".

Moments earlier, after his second smash of the day, Dennis had spotted something that he thought might come in useful. He'd crashed near the scrapyard magnet. (Remember that from right at the start?) Recalling what his dad had told him –

that magnets can mess up electronics – Dennis felt sure that having it would somehow help. I mean, spaceships have got electronics, right?

There were two things connected to the magnet: the power supply and the cable.

The power feed, once unplugged from the crane, easily plugged into a spare port on the side of the attack fighter.

The cable was a bigger problem. It was properly attached to Walter's crane, even though the winch was broken.

Dennis had searched his ship for a handheld laser blaster, but found nothing, and the stupid ship wasn't pointing in the right direction for its lasers to work.

"Gnasher!" Dennis had exclaimed. "Your teeth are tougher than Wolverine's claws. I need you to bite through this cable!"

Gnasher was more than unsure.

"I've shredded countless posties' pants.

Chewed through fences. Gnawed through bony chops, gnashed car bumpers... but never a steel cable!" he said.

He loved his gnashy gnashers. They were who he was.

Dennis placed his hands either side of Gnasher's air mask, ready to take it off. "You don't have to if you don't want to, but what would Captain Star Paws do?" he asked Gnasher.

Gnasher thought for a moment. He couldn't think of another way. Nervously, Gnasher agreed. He took a big gulp of air and Dennis took off his air mask. Gnasher quickly opened his powerful jaws and...

GNASH!

The cable broke! Cut clean in two! Gnasher's gnashy gnashers had saved the day!

A moment later, Dennis and Gnasher were flying back into the fight with a huge electromagnet dangling underneath their ship.

Well, to be truthful, it was a bit more than a moment. Getting the ship started again took quite a bit of shouting and kicking the dash, but Dennis had managed it in the end.

Dennis didn't know why the drones were attacking the executive fighter, but he knew that if they succeeded in destroying the ship that controlled them, there would be no way to steer Beanotown back.

Dennis switched on the magnet and zipped over the top of Walter's ship.

KUNG!!!

The magnet grabbed hold of the executive fighter, and everything on board went haywire! Sparks and little lightning bolts jumped from the dash as Walter pulled his hands away.

"WHAT'S GOING ON NOW?" he asked no one in particular.

Every drone dropped out of the sky and clattered into the flying part of Beanotown.

Dennis winced, as did Minnie when she saw them drop.

"I hope they're alright," Gnasher said.

Something else that tried to drop out of the sky was Walter's ship. It fell a bit, but soon stopped because it was still connected to Dennis's ship by the magnet and cable.

Slowly, Dennis lowered Walter's ship to the ground, and turned off the magnet.

Dennis and Gnasher landed and ran over, just as Minnie stood up triumphant on Walter's ship

"I did it!" she exclaimed. "I brought down Walter's fighter and saved the town!"

"*I* brought the fighter down, and nothing's been saved yet!" said Dennis, pointing to the edge of the town. There was fire all around them from the burning fallen drones.

"We're coming back through the atmosphere!" Gnasher said.

"Cool!" said Minnie. "We'll have air soon... Wait. You can talk? And you sound like..." Minnie suddenly realised the dashing and handsome space captain she'd been imagining was Dennis's dog.

"The town's about to smash into Earth like the asteroid that got rid of the dinosaurs, destroying the town and sending Earth into a decades-long winter."

"So, some good, some bad?" said Minnie.

Walter was desperately trying to restart the battered ship he was in. Dennis opened the cockpit.

"Walter!" Dennis shouted. "There's no time for you to save your parents and keep this ship! It's destroyed now anyway! The only hope for all of us is to save the entire town!"

Walter saw the growing fire round the edge of the town, as Beanotown burned its way back into Earth's atmosphere. He groaned. "Urrrgh! I guess you're right! I can't do anything with this thing though! You broke it with your magnet!" Walter wrestled with the controls, but all that happened was the dashboard flashed confusingly.

"There's only one thing for it..." Minnie said.

"Turn it off and on again!" Gnasher finished.

"ARRRRGH! Your dog can talk!" Walter exclaimed.

"Duh!" said Dennis. "Catch up!" He pointed to Walter's dash. "Where's the off button?"

Walter found the off button and pressed it. Everything turned off. He went to turn it back on, but Dennis grabbed his hand to stop him.

"You're meant to wait five seconds," he said.

"That five-second thing's a load of rubbish!" said Minnie as she noticed bushes and trees coming loose from the edge of Beanotown and seemingly floating upwards, as Beanotown plummeted down to Earth.

"Right, well that was five seconds!" Walter said, and pressed the on button.

Nothing happened.

FISHING? CRASHING! WISHING?

Over in Dennis's house, and across Beanotown, a similar scene was playing out: a lot of gasping. They were running out of air.

Dad panicked most and clawed at his makeshift helmet. Knowing that there was even less air outside their suits, Mum called Dad an idiot. Dad was panicking and breathing way more than his fair share.

"Stop that!" Mum shouted at her idiot husband. "Calm down."

Then baby Bea let rip with the stinkiest pump of her life.

As they were all sharing air, Mum panicked too and all three Menaces clawed their way out of their suits and pods.

They were fully expecting to breathe in huge gulps of nothing, but had decided anything was better than one of Bea's guffiest guffs.

But there was air! Sweet, sweet – if still a little thin – air!

Dad laughed.

"It's back!" he cried. **"The air's back! We're all safe!"**

Almost daily, Dad was wrong about something. This was the wrongest he'd ever been. This was the furthest from safe they'd ever been!

Back at the executive fighter, the dash continued to do nothing.

"Try it again!" Gnasher urged. "You didn't press it right!"

"No, don't!" Dennis warned. "You'll just be turning it off again!"

PING!

The ship's controls came back on again.

Dennis, Gnasher and Walter all shouted at the computer at the same time. They all told it to reactivate the drones and position them round the edge of Beanotown to slow the town's descent. But they all said it in slightly different ways, so it was impossible to tell what any of them said.

"I'm sorry," said the onboard computer. "I didn't quite catch that. Would you mind repeating it?"

Minnie jammed her hands over the boys' mouths.

"Wake up all drones and use them to stop this town crashing!" she said.

"How do I stop the town washing?" the computer asked.

"Crashing!" Minnie shouted.

"Fishing?" asked the computer.

"Crashing!"

"Wishing?"

Dennis and Walter pulled Minnie's hands away, and all four of them, Gnasher included, shouted: **"CRASHING!!!"**

"Yes. I can try to stop the town crashing," the computer said, as all around them the sleeping drones woke up and flew off in different directions.

All three children and the dog thought "try?!", and looked nervously at each other.

Back on Earth, (that still sounds good) the inhabitants of Beanotown who were left on Earth looked up into the sky and saw the rest of the town returning. Even though it was still quite far away, they could see that several of the jets keeping it in the sky were no longer working.

With a PUTT PUTT PUTT! another jet stopped working, and another.

With every jet that stopped, Beanotown got bigger and bigger in the sky.

Oh, thought some of the more knowledgable townsfolk. At that speed, when Beanotown hits Earth, everything for miles around will be utterly obliterated. And they kinda wished they weren't so knowledgeable.

Then a tiny jet appeared and activated underneath the town. From down on the ground it was impossible to see why or where it had come from.

Then another, and another.

As the last of the 10 huge jets went out, more and more of these tiny jets – the drones – turned on. There were almost a hundred of them.

But was the power of nearly a hundred little jets the same as the power from 10 huge jets? The world was about to find out.

Back on the (extremely large) bit of Beanotown that was falling out of the sky, Dennis and Gnasher saw the edge of the world rise to meet them. The familiar horizon was returning, if a little quicker than anyone would hope. They could feel the town slowing the same way you can feel a car slowing when inside it, but was it enough?

Dennis started a countdown, **"TEN, NINE, EIGHT..."**

BOOM!

SNEAKY MANOEUVRES

Beanotown landed back in the hole it'd left only a short time ago, and everyone was thrown off their feet. (Apart from Gnasher, who had a leg at each corner.) Walter was thrown out of his ship.

Dennis was the first to stand back up and dust himself off. "I was a bit off with my timing there," he admitted.

"Gno, really?" Gnasher said.

And that's the story of how Walter saved Beanotown.

"WHAT?!" I hear you shout.

"WALTER WAS GOING TO LET BEANOTOWN BE DESTROYED!" I hear you cry.

But technically he was the one who turned the computer in the executive fighter off and on again. Plus, he was the first one to get to a reporter and say "I saved the town!", and people tend to believe the first thing they hear. You can tell them "Well, actually..." all you want. Most people will still stick with the "fact" they hear first, whether it's true or not.

Quietly, in the background, Walter was assessing the executive fighter. It was badly damaged, but nothing he couldn't have someone fix up. All the drones were squashed under Beanotown. But with an attack fighter like this one, he could still strike fear into the hearts of everyone in town.

I'll have to be quick, he thought to himself. The second I get it going, I need to destroy Dennis's fighter, before he has a chance to get in it!

Behind Dennis, Gnasher and Minnie's back, he crept back to the fighter he'd been thrown from moments ago, and...

... saw Lady BigBad sitting in the pilot's seat. (That's why the teleport doesn't make a sound. It's for sneaky manoeuvres like this one.) She looked at Walter with a sly grin.

"I know what you were going to do," she said. "And I can't help but like you for it, but this is mine!"

And with that, the executive, but seriously smashed-in, fighter took off for the city ship.

Walter's heart sank for a moment. Then he realised Dennis's fighter was still there!

He ran over to it and saw Ploop sitting in the pilot's seat.

Ploop looked at him and said, "What she said!", then took off for the city ship herself.

Dennis, Gnasher, Minnie and Walter watched as the two alien aircraft zipped away.

"Gnash!" said Gnasher.

Dennis turned to him. "Buddy! Are you back to normal?!"

But, as everyone knows, there's no such thing as normal in Beanotown.

Dennis looked up to the fighter ships which were already little more than dots in the sky. The translators that allowed Dennis to understand his faithful hound were now too far away to work.

"Gnash!" Gnasher gnashed. He shrugged. Ah well, he thought. Easy come, easy go.

Dennis was secretly a bit glad. Talking Gnasher was kind of cheeky and sounded cleverer than him.

Dennis looked around and frowned. "I was going to say 'let's go home', but how do we do that?" he asked Gnasher.

You see, when Beanotown landed back in the

Can you find the way home for Dennis and Gnasher? Starting from star, finishing at the letter D.

hole, it hadn't landed perfectly. It was the right way up, but none of the roads lined up. All around town, roads stopped dead in the middle of gardens, or ran straight into the sides of houses. So, as bad as things used to be trying to find your way round town, it was ten times worse now.

Things got back to normal pretty quickly in Beanotown...

As if! Three days later, through an unlikely

chain of events, Gnasher was turned into a giant dog. The day after that, Mayor Wilbur burst out of his safe in the town hall, having finally run out of air.

Oh, he wondered. How long have we been back on Earth?

A few days after that, Walter was given superpowers, also through an unlikely chain of events. And near the end of the month, no one could figure out why Minnie's hair turned blue. Like I say, "normal" – for Beanotown at least!

On the BigBad Alliance's city ship, things never quite got back to normal. The most popular form of entertainment had always been the battle arena, but now its popularity really took off.

Minnie's battle partner, Kurg, and the other "fighters" were now superstars. Their faces were on everything from lunchboxes to T-shirts. How could they not be? It was all so much more fun now.

And, strangely, that fun seemed to infect everything else on the city ship. Aliens started enjoying their day-to-day lives much more and tried to have more fun in general. Even Lady BigBad started to crack jokes! If you didn't laugh, she'd have you ejected into space, so people tended to laugh quite a bit.

THE END

"The end!" said Dennis, smiling broadly.

"Finally," said Santa, standing up. "Took long enough!"

He turned to address Dennis and tapped his wrist where people used to wear watches. "We're on a clock, you know!"

"Oh yeah," Dennis replied, remembering. "The thing with the thing!"

Santa looked round. "Where's Prancer?" he asked.

"I think he's in my kitchen," I answered.

And he was. He'd done a poo and was eating my cornflakes.